Praise for A *Spring That Did Not Blossom*

"Skillfully and intelligently, this book memorializes the forgotten victims and martyrs of the Palestinian refugee camps in Lebanon, from forty years ago. It conveys the event to us quietly, without noise, chatter, slogans, glorifications or calls for revenge. We do not find in it the resonant speeches, the rhetorical constructions, or even the false linguistic metaphors that undertake elaborate explanations which distance us from the tragic truth it all leads to—the path to massacre."
—Aqeel Manqoush, *Thaqafat*

"The book is a testimony to the suffering of the Palestinian people in Lebanon at the beginning of the civil war and up to the Israeli invasion. It brings back to memory scenes of the pervasive massacres of refugees in Palestinian camps, including the events of the camps of Dbayeh, Sabra and Shatila, and the siege of the capital, Beirut."
—*Al-Quds al-Arabi*

"[A] collection of stories whose protagonists are fictionalized versions of real people, perhaps the most prominent of which is the child Rabih [which means 'Spring' in English], who was killed along with his family on August 6 [1982] as a result of the vacuum bomb dropped by Israeli planes on the Aker apartment buildir inhabited by many Palestinian families displaced from the Dbayeh refugee camp. Hence, the name of the novel, *A Spring that Did Not Blossom*, is in memory of Rabih, the child who died before he had a chance to bloom."

—*SBS Arabic*

"Nejmeh Khalil Habib is a literary critic of high calibre, whose moral fibre coincides with her being a pioneer in human rights, justice, and freedom."

—Izzat Abdulhadi, Palestine Ambassador to Australia, New Zealand and the Pacific

"...a distinct and smooth narrative style."

—Hassan Ghanaam

"[A] skilful documentation of an era in Palestinian resistance and perseverance."

—George Hashem

"Reminiscent of the telegraphic style of Ghassan Kanafani ... brevity generates a sense of hurriedness ... a beautifully crafted work of art, which also stands as an artefact of substantial historical and cultural import."

—Samar Habib

"A book that deserves to be known and read worldwide."

—Nouha Francis

A SPRING THAT DID NOT BLOSSOM

PALESTINIAN SHORT STORIES

By Nejmeh Khalil Habib
Translated by Samar Habib

Interlink Books
An imprint of Interlink Publishing Group, Inc.
Northampton, Massachusetts

First published in 2024 by

Interlink Books
An imprint of Interlink Publishing Group, Inc.
46 Crosby Street, Northampton, MA 01060
www.interlinkbooks.com

Originally published in Arabic as *Rabi'on Lam Yuzhir* by Arab
Scientific Publishers, Beirut, Lebanon

Library of Congress Cataloging-in-Publication data:
ISBN-13: 978-1-62371-663-9

Printed and bound in the United States of America

CONTENTS

Here is the silver birdbath
And here's the bird bathing
This one caught it
That one slayed it
Another roasted it
This one ate it
And that one said:
Tweet, tweet, tweet, tweet

—A children's nursery rhyme

MARIAM

An elderly stout woman, dressed in a loose garment with hair tied back with a thin bandana, claps her veiny hands. She succeeds in planting a kiss on her grandson's cheek moments before he squeezes his way out of her arms. She gives him a cream-filled treat in exchange for permission to kiss him, but even this fails to persuade him. His mother's kisses were nicer and she smelled better.

"Rabih[1] is a gazelle," he says, extricating himself from her embrace.

"Rabih is a donkey," she chimes back

"No, gazelle!"

"Donkey!"

....

1   Rabih is both a boy's name and the Arabic word for "spring." The collection's title plays with the connotations of the word "spring" as it pertains to both "the Arab spring" and the blossoming the spring season usually heralds.

"Gazelle! Gazelle!" Rabih shouts, striking her lap with both fists, demanding she admit that he is, after all, a gazelle.

They had named him Rabih to reflect the good omen of his birth. Neither his mother nor father had expected they would have children. They were both past childbearing age when he was conceived, and the event, therefore, sprinkled the desert of their existence with a gentle and promising rain.

His birth softened his father, who lived a rough and solitary life prior to his arrival. Rabih's mother found in him the solace she had been deprived of in her youth. His dreamy eyes, which looked like his grandfather's, were her whole world: past, present and future.

Heart filled with optimistic expectations, his father gave him the title of "Abu Awad"[2] before he could even speak his first word.

"No one names their son 'Awad' nowadays," Mariam interjected.

"I don't care what names people use. He's my son, and I'm free to call him whatever I want."

"No, darling, the proverb says eat what you like and wear what other people like."

"What sophistry! The man makes his name!"

....

2   It is customary among Arab families to name a man as the father of his eldest son. By calling Rabih "Abu Awad," Awad is intimating that Rabih will one day name his own oldest son after him, thus becoming "Abu Awad."

There's no point talking to him, he's so dense, Mariam thinks to herself.

"If names cost money, everyone's name would be Shit."

Im Awad[3] sits silently as usual, her facial features set to neutral, betraying neither approval nor disapproval.

I don't know how Abu Awad put up with her all his life, or how he had a dozen children with her. God rest his soul.

Mariam's delight in Rabih had been hyperbolic. He was, after all, the fruit of a womb she thought was barren. She lit candles in Rabih's name at every nearby shrine and church, asking God to protect him from the evil eye. And the day his first tooth appeared, she made and delivered plates of *snuniyeh*[4] to all the houses in the camp.

"She didn't make as big of a deal on our wedding day as she's making now."

"If the situation wasn't so bad, I would've made *ouzi*[5] instead of wheat."

....

3 Similarly to the logic of the previous footnote, *Im Awad* means "the mother of Awad."

4 This is a dessert made of boiled wheat, decorated with nuts and chocolate, it is prepared and distributed among neighbors and relatives in celebration of the appearance of a child's first tooth.

5 A banquet-style centerpiece consisting of boiled rice and topped with pieces of lamb. It is usually served at big occasions like marriages. The serving of meat usually denotes a position of wealth for the host family.

And the day he was baptized, she practically turned it into a wedding.

"What are we going to do for an actual wedding now?" Awad asked. She glanced at her husband crossly, murmured a few words to herself and went on as planned. She knew he wasn't entirely serious in his complaint, that all he really wanted was to ruffle her feathers a little. His eyes betrayed the childlike happiness he tried to conceal.

He has a good heart, like the heart of a child. But he thinks that showing love and affection breaks a man's stature and hurt his pride.

Rabih came into this world during a dark time in the history of the region. He was born a few months before the Ain al-Rumaneh bus massacre.[6] So, it was while he was taking his first steps that the earthquake of wrath hit the tiny camp he was born in. And so those who could flee, fled. And those who could not, died. The surviving few became whatever their captors needed them to be.

"We, sweetheart," Mariam explained to Awad, "are sometimes hostages, sometimes enemies, sometimes scapegoats, and sometimes just a punching bag for anyone who wants to let off some steam."

....

6　In April 1975, gunmen from the Lebanese Phalangist militia opened fire on a bus carrying mostly Palestinian passengers as it made its way through the Beirut suburb of Ain al-Rumaneh. The ambush killed most of the passengers. This and similar clashes marked the beginning of the Lebanese civil war.

Abu Rabih was in one of the Gulf countries,[7] running after his livelihood, when the camp fell into the hands of one of the militias. He was horrified. He got the news of his relatives and neighbors who were massacred: his brother-in-law, Rafful, who was taken from his home and never heard of or seen again; his neighbor, Shiya, who was crushed by a tank; Abu Bushara's daughter, who was raped and burned; and the children, all below the age of sixteen, who were executed on the outskirts of the camp. But Abu Rabih was consoled by the fact that Rabih and his mother were among the few who were stung but not burned.

Mariam noticed her husband had returned a different man. His voice had become gentler, and his general gruffness had subsided.

"You are a queen among women, Mariam. A sister of men, wallah! I pray that I may be able to recompense you for all you endured on your own."

"Don't worry, Abu Rabih, I was able to handle it all."

"It was against my will, Mariam. If I could've come back, I wouldn't have stayed even one hour after I heard the news."

Mariam continued to stare at the ground, silent. He wondered if she doubted him:

"You know the airport was closed, and it

7 Palestinian refugees to this day continue to seek gainful employment in countries of the Arab Gulf. The trend began after the creation of the Palestinian refugee crisis in 1948.

would've been crazy to come back on a ship with my travel document[8]—it's like a crime to have one of these nowadays."

"I thanked God a thousand times because you were away," she replied with a cloud of sadness drifting through her eyes. "Everything was going to happen, with or without your presence. You couldn't have done anything ... Who knows. Maybe if you had been here, they might've taken you too, like everyone else they took."

"Are you sure they're gone? Atta, Rafful, Abu Nabeel and the others? Are you sure? Can't they just be detained?"

"After all this time? I doubt it. Poor Atta. He broke his mother's heart. She didn't get to see him, or say goodbye. Nobody knows how he died. Did the vultures get to eat him, or the fish? Poor Atta, he longed to die in Palestine. Look how he died at the hands of people who have nothing to do with Palestine and with whom we have no quarrel."

Abu Rabih had only been back a few hours when he heard a voice say, "The boss wants to see you." He

....

8   Even to this day, Palestinians in Lebanon are not allowed to have a passport; instead, they may travel only with a travel document issued specifically for Palestinian refugees in Lebanon. During the civil war, Palestinians were afraid to disclose their status at checkpoints or other points of entry because many right-wing militias considered them enemies of the state, and executions just for being Palestinian became commonplace.

knew the request was meant for him. "Be there in half an hour."

"Oh, Mother Mary, what does he want?" Mariam spoke nervously, wringing her hands.

"Relax, woman. What do they want? They want money."

"Money? Money! Haven't they taken enough? Every other day they knock on the door: contribution, alms, donations ... Damn this life!"

In a room that had been, months earlier, an office for the Palestinian armed resistance, sat a man behind a desk, who, with some fundamental changes in clichés, was nonetheless not that different from his predecessor. He was a little shorter, his skin was lighter and his moustache thicker. But he and his predecessor both enjoyed whatever that table endowed them of additional benefits over God's other creatures.

"Are you Awad?" He asked without lifting his gaze from the desk.

"Yes, sir."

"Where were you all this time?"

"I was in Abu Dhabi."

"Abu Dhabi, are you sure? Not in Syria, maybe, where you were training with the hoodlums?"

"I swear on your life, sir, I have no connections with hoodlums nor with Bashas. I've been in the Gulf for twenty years. Every now and then I come back to visit the family for a month or two."

"Don't think that you can pull the wool over our eyes. We have eyes and ears everywhere. If we didn't know you were clean, you never would've made it back to your house. Tell me, what did you do in West Beirut? You didn't come straight from the airport, correct?"

"That's correct, sir. I spent the night at my brother's house. He lives in Ras Beirut."

"Your brother? Your brother! We didn't know you had a brother in West Beirut!"

"He's been living there for a long time. Since he got married. His wife is Beiruti. She thinks she's too good for the camp. They only visit us on important occasions."

"And does your brother have any hoodlum friends?"

"Oh sir, if my brother did, you'd be the first to know. He only knows his job and his home. His wife never stops cursing armed men."

"And how did you find West Beirut?"

"Garbage. Traffic. Chaos. Roaming merchants everywhere, no order or organization. Hamra is not what it used to be."

"Hamra deserves what happened to it. It took in these vandals and they turned it into a slum." He kept his gaze fixed on the ground while the boss continued, "Shame on you, Awad! I thought you had better manners. How could you come back without dropping by to say 'hi' and to thank us for keeping your mother, wife and son safe?"

"Ah ... sir ..."

"What do you take us for? A charitable organization? An oil well? The United Nations? A relief agency? We protect you and stay up at night, while you rest ... do you think it's fair to expect all of that for free?"

"I ... I'm sorry sir. I ... I ... there is no ... it slipped my mind."

He reached into his pocket, took out a few bank notes and placed them on the table in front of him.

"Would you like anything else, sir?"

The boss gestured for him to get out. Awad got up and turned to leave.

"We were hoping you'd be a bit more generous. At any rate, you can do better next time."

Awad swallowed and tapped his pockets with his hands.

He headed home, head hanging, forlorn, but when the smell of Mariam's famous *kibbe* reached him, he felt his spirits lighten a little.

The boy started to get used to his father. He stopped hiding behind his mother every time Awad tried to reach for him. Instead, he actively sought his father's attention, laughing loudly every time Awad tickled him. It was this laughter that bubbled in Awad's veins, filling him with a strange joy, the likes of which he had never felt before. He took such pleasure in Rabih, it almost intoxicated him, and he felt something unusual for Mariam. Was it love? At this age, could it be? Was it a feeling of companionship? The feeling that there was someone you could say "I'm sad" to, when you were sad, and "I'm happy" to, when you were happy? Someone who could help you bear the weight of your oppression in these dark times?

The day he married her, he felt like he was carrying out an obligation to his mother, to keep her happy. His friend Mahmood had another theory. He said that loneliness had eaten him up after all those years trekking between Kuwait, Bahrain, Qatar and the Emirates, finally making his way to Baghdad and Mosul. All his friends, and even his younger siblings, got married and had kids, so he had no excuses left for his mother.

"A wife is good support for a man. She protects him from loose women. She saves his money. She meets his needs. A woman completes a man."

"I don't need a woman to complete me. God created me complete. I can save my own money, and I have no interest in loose women. I've lived in so many different countries for twenty years—I've learned to cook, clean and iron my clothes. Talk about something else, ya Im Awad." But this time, he was actually joking, teasing her. He enjoyed getting her all riled up, watching as she struggled to keep her anger from showing.

Concerned for the distress he saw in her eyes,

he said, "Don't worry Im Awad, I won't go back overseas until I'm a married man. What do you say to that?"

She knelt on the floor and kissed it.

He picked Mariam because they were around the same age. She too had "missed the boat." In the spring of her youth, when a young woman's appetite for marriage and love flowers, she was busy feeding the mouths of little children, which her own refugee father, who knew no trade, was unable to do. By the time she raised her siblings, her opportunities for marriage had become virtually nonexistent. She was approaching forty, which was why she didn't hesitate for a moment to say yes. The oldest of her brothers objected to the marriage.

"A marriage like that is going to imprison you, Mariam. Awad? Awad! Of all the men in the world, he's the one who's going to be my brother-in-law? I've never seen him with a friend. He's a harsh and hard-headed man, who has lived away from his family for all these years. That's probably what made him so gruff. You'll be in exile with him, and if God blesses you with a child, he'll be too old to raise him. He's over forty; you're not a young woman anymore either."

She listened but didn't comment. He hadn't said anything she didn't already know, but the agony of being a spinster was the worst of all exiles and prisons. And who knew what the future held? God was generous, maybe marriage would change him. Everyone in the camp talked about Atef—how he was before he got married and how he became afterward.

"Not Awad, Mariam. Not him. Awad won't change, he's carved from stone."

"Let me try my luck. Anything is better than the situation I'm in now. You will all get married and get busy with your wives and children soon. In a few years, the factory will retire me, and then I'll be either a burden on you or a maid for your families. Maybe God will have mercy on me and grant me a child of my own. It would be the greatest recompense of my life. God is great. He raises us all."

It was a swift marriage between two older people who feared missing out on having, like almost everyone in creation, a house, family and children.

Love did not ignite between them to melt the contradictions in their personalities, but a common trauma united them: each had survived the Palestinian Nakba as a child, bore its lacerations and felt loneliness as they got older.

While he was closed in on himself, she had a few modest friendships to sustain her, along with some political interests and opinions on life she gathered from disparate sources, influenced by an educated brother and a sister who had richer life experiences through study and work.

Her sex education came from articles published

in *Al Hasnaa* Magazine.

He married her in haste. No preludes or engagements. He bought for them a recently built apartment in the camp. It was an elegant home without either excess or miserliness. Mariam was pleased with her new home. She hung curtains she'd had for several years, and even though they had begun to yellow, she insisted on showing them off. Her kitchen, despite it being small, was a gallery for all kinds of embroidery, which led Awad to question whether it was a kitchen or an embroidery shop.

She'd wink at her guests while he wasn't looking, making light of his ignorance and lack of appreciation.

"When the little bub arrives, all of these will become rubbish," he'd say in a playfully cautionary way.

Is it true that there will be a little bub? Is it really possible for her to get pregnant at this age? She's almost forty. But God is great. She'd known of many women who had stayed fertile even after forty. She had a few years left, and she wasn't greedy. Just one child would be enough.

Mariam's womb was indeed fertile, unperturbed by years of disuse. Within a few months she was pregnant. It was the happiest feeling she had ever felt in her life. She would never forget the first few kicks her fetus made against the wall of her stomach, and she told that story and of the effect it had on her until her last breath.

As Mariam's midsection got bigger, she spent the days feeling it with her hands and talking to the fetus. Singing to it. Grabbing the hand of whoever was nearby, asking, "Can you feel him kicking? Can you feel how energetic he is?"

She spent her entire pregnancy preparing for his arrival. The whole operation was the talk of the camp. His nursery became an exhibit for all sorts of textiles and dentelle, so much so that her neighbors began to mock her behind her back:

It's like it's the first pregnancy in history.

It's as though the forthcoming heir is the Prince of Believers,[9] *or the conqueror of Andalusia.*[10]

Say "the son of Mariam, blessed be her name."[11]

Mariam was oblivious of their derision, preoccupied with the angelic pulse that only women who have fallen pregnant late in life would know the value of. Her greatest wish at that time was that the child be born a boy, so that Awad's happiness would be complete.

Mariam felt that the world could barely contain

....

9   Translated literally here from the Arabic *Emir al-Mu'mineen*, the Prince of Believers, is an honorary title, often translated as Commander of the Faithful. It was first conferred upon the Caliph Omar Ibn Khattab.

10   Abd al-Raham the First, who brought Islamic reign to southern Spain in the eighth century.

11   Mariam is the Arabic name for Mary. Evidently the neighbor is derisively referring to the Virgin Mary and her son, Jesus.

her joy. Everything in existence was laughing: the father who was carved from stone, the yelling of the neighborhood children, her mother-in-law's awful comments, even the fishmonger's piercing and insistent shouting—all of these things became causes for joy, calls for happiness.

Every now and then, she'd complain about the husband who deprived her of the pleasure of idle conversation.

"Awad huffs and puffs every time an old friend comes to visit me. He goes dumb if we run into my father in the street and I invite him up for a coffee. Drinking and sleeping are all that he cares for in this world. Even when he tries to romance me, he says 'Mariam is a great cook!' He even wants me to be grateful for his virility: 'What happened to you wouldn't even happen to a fourteen-year-old!'" Mariam would soon recognize, however, that her unborn child compensated for all the ills of her entire life. She recognized that unlike many others, she did not suffer neither great humiliation nor a tremendous sacrifice, and for these reasons she did not let Awad's comments affect her.

She was overjoyed the day Rabih was born. She sent plates of *mighli*[12] to her neighbors, friends and relatives—those who cared and those who didn't alike. Of course Awad objected to the matter when he found out, but she ignored him.

12 Mighli is a cinnamon-flavored rice pudding, topped with nuts and sweets, offered to visitors coming to congratulate the mother on the birth of a new child.

Weeks passed since Awad's return, and with every heartbeat he too rejoiced in his fatherhood. He was so filled with Rabih's presence that he felt himself becoming smaller and smaller, so small in fact, that he thought he just might be able to fly with, or jump after, the butterflies. Sometimes he played peek-a-boo with him, and sometimes they played hide-and-seek, he even deigned to crawl on all fours with Rabih on his back, calling out with joy, "Move, move, ya donkey!"

Awad's days were spent running after Rabih's paper planes, or escorting him to the nearby corner store to stock up on sweets and sodas. Whenever Mariam objected angrily, Awad would whisper something in his son's ear and they would both burst out laughing and continue on their way, paying her no heed.

Awad was very happy with his family and yet he felt pained at the loss of many of his neighbors, relatives and friends. He did his best to adapt to the new reality and built superficial relationships with his new neighbors, who had fled the persecution of the other side. As far as he was concerned, these new neighbors were in the end also victims, just like his own people.[13]

He got used to the caustic feeling of being forced
....

13 After the fall of the camp, many Palestinian homes were
     confiscated and given to Lebanese families that supported
     the Phalangists, many of these families had been
     displaced from other regions due to the ongoing fighting.

to do something he didn't want to do. He even got used to soothing Mariam's rage every time she had to make a donation she didn't want to make: "It's OK ... as long as we can afford to pay the ransom, we should."

"We're scapegoats! A half-eaten loaf of cornbread!"[14]

"God will deliver us, *ya bint al-halal*."[15]

"We're hostages here, discarded leaves of a tree. Why don't we go to West Beirut, join the rest of our people there?"

"Who says West Beirut is any better? At least here we know what to expect, but over there every day is a surprise: Israel at one end, some organization or other at the other ... Be patient. They'll get bored in time and leave us alone. These are tough times for everyone, and they too shall pass."

"Lives pass too."

"There are housing shortages in West Beirut. We couldn't buy an apartment with all the savings we have, not even one that's likely to be condemned or invaded at any moment. Be patient, dear Mariam. Patience is the key to salvation."

"Rabih is all alone here, without any of his cousins to play with. How unlucky you are, ya Rabih! If only you'd come before this dark and miserable time. He doesn't have an aunt to play with him, or a cousin to tell him stories, or a neighbor to cuddle him."

....

14 Cornbread is considered inferior to bread made with wheat.

15 An expression referring to a woman as virtuous.

Awad was killing time with a game of backgammon with one of his neighbors—a man who, under different circumstances, would have been unlikely to do so much as offer a morning greeting. But here they were now, conversing between throws of the dice.

"You are lucky, Abu Rabih, not just in backgammon but in life as well. Very lucky that you weren't here that night of tremendous madness."

"Well, that night of madness was harder on me than anyone else. When you're with your family, you know what's happening to them, minute by minute, but when you're away, you go crazy between contacts. I could've killed someone that night!"

"Whoa! To that extent?"

"I swear, brother Tayim, I could've killed ..."

Tayim didn't throw his dice; instead he stared into Awad's eyes, anxious for more details.

"My nerves were so frayed. I couldn't even handle a fly if it landed. And then some son of a bitch got up and started theorizing and giving advice. He said that our camp was full of traitors. He said we betrayed the revolution. Is it true that we betrayed the revolution, brother Tayim? I heard that the revolution betrayed us. They're the ones who filled the heads of young men with hot air, telling them that if a battle broke out, they'd subsidize us, that they'd join in from Sabra...[16] Is that true?"

....

16   Sabra is the site of a Palestinian refugee camp in West Beirut.

"True or not, it doesn't matter anymore. Go on, Abu Rabih, please tell me more."

"You know I'm not good at talking, so I got out of my seat and grabbed him by the neck and shouted, 'Screw you and your revolution! You all come off the bottom of my shoe. The only thing I care about is my wife and kid. I pray that Israel invades you, not just the Phalangists!' I would have strangled him if the others hadn't intervened and separated us. Brother Tayim, they got to eat the chickens and we ended up in the cage. They did what they did and ran away, leaving us to suffer the consequences on their behalf."

"You didn't see what happened, Abu Rabih. People had to choose either between fleeing or dying. I feel sorry for this camp. It was a model for all the other camps. Our brothers used to call it a bourgeois camp."

"There was nothing bourgeois about it. Just a few outward pretenses. Some families bought washing machines or refrigerators—that's what they call bourgeois."

"Your friend Abu Ahmad ... Abu Ahmad, no other! The head of the resistance, he used to say *mashalla*, your daughters are like the women in Hamra, fashionably dressed to meet up with their boyfriends behind the church.'"

"Bless his heart! Back in the day his mother used to meet boys on her way to the spring well. By God, if it weren't for Abu George, the rats would have eaten us ... These boxes of cement they call houses are called rabbit warrens in other countries!"

"No, brother Awad, you are mistaken. Our camp in the old days was something to be proud of. It was the only camp that had a school with a baccalaureate. And its location! The views from here are spectacular. People lived like they were one big family."

"They never lived like they were one big family. They argued over a water can and a few centimeters of land that wasn't even theirs. They bit into each other's flesh like wolves. The people of our camp lost their piety, they became dissipated. That's why what happened, happened."

"Speaking of losing piety, where do you think Nicholas's infidel soul went?"

"Nicholas? His soul is still trapped under the rubble of his coffee house, which they[17] demolished over his head. It's as if I can still hear him tell his obscene jokes and play his pranks on the religious people of the neighborhood."

"He was the biggest infidel. Are you a believer, Abu Rabih?"

"Honestly, I don't know. Believer, infidel. Coward, reasonable. Bad, good. I don't know what I am."

They heard the voice of a man nicknamed Deek[18] from a distance.

....

17 The Phalangists

18 The Arabic word for rooster.

"In the absence of manhood, al-Deek's become Abu Ali,"[19] Tayim said under his breath.

"They say that the underground tunnels[20] were full of weapons and foreign fighters," Awad remarked.

"Bullshit! Everyone knows the camp has been empty since the war between the freedom fighters and the army in 1973. They know every tomato plant in this camp. Had they suspected they would meet with any resistance, they wouldn't have dared to start a fight over something so trivial. They had eyes and ears among us, more than there are fleas in the lentil rations.[21] I wouldn't be surprised if you, brother Awad, weren't an informant on me, keeping tabs on what I say and reporting it," Tayim laughed.

"Is it true they detained Somalis in the camp?"

"How could you believe such bullshit? If there had been real fighters here, would they have been able to invade the camp in less than forty-eight hours?"

....

19 The proverb *al-deek sar Abu Ali* means that in the absence of strong men, men of lesser stature (who are referred to as roosters) take on a position of sovereignty over others, which they do not deserve.

20 The French army dug these tunnels under a hill adjacent to the camp at some point during its mandate.

21 The camp received humanitarian aid in the form of food and other essential supplies from the United Nations Relief and Works Agency. It would often take these rations a long time to be distributed, and grains like lentils or rice often had to be sifted through to remove fleas before being used.

"They say that Abu Bashara's daughter was in a romantic relationship with a man from the resistance. They say he's the one who raped and then burned her alive, not them."

"Lies. No one in their right mind would believe this stuff. A story like that is only possible in *A Thousand and One Nights*."

"This is such a vile war."

"You talk like comrade Omar did in his day, may God rest his soul. When has war ever been anything but vile, huh? Give a mother, in her tomb, some guns, and she too will turn into Antar.[22] If your Jesus had access to guns, he never would've said, 'If anyone slaps you on the right cheek, turn to him the other cheek.'"

A voice came and went. He heard, "Tell Awad that the boss wants to see him in his office immediately."

Awad looked at his neighbor meaningfully, closed the backgammon table, pushed off his knees with his palms and shuffled his way to the boss's office.

The boss's voice met him forcefully. "It looks like fresh air has done you wonders, Awad! Praised be! Praised be! There is nothing better than good health. What do you think of the camp now, Awad? Prettier, isn't it, now that the assholes have left?"

. . . .

22 Antarah Ibn Shadad al-Absi, the illegitimate son of the chief of one of the largest tribes in pre-Islamic Arabia. He was claimed by his father only after developing a reputation for being a fierce and unbeatable warrior.

He remained silent.

"Did you hear about the battle at Matan,[23] Awad?"

The color drained from his face and he wondered silently what might be behind such a prelude. Was the boss going to take him to the frontlines? Use him to exact revenge on the enemy? Awad tried to engage in niceties but nothing substantial came out of his mouth. The boss soon continued, without looking at his prisoner:

"In short, we need blood. We have a lot of injured and our men have a right over us. It's the duty of everyone who lives in this neighborhood to help. They're spending all their blood for our sake. You and your likes in this camp have to prove that you support us, that you are one of us."

He returned home and threw himself on the bed. She spoke to him but he didn't answer. She repeated her question, followed by a reprimand for keeping them in their existing living arrangement, but he remained silent. She resorted to her usual trick: preparing a cup of coffee, the smell of which usually snapped him out of his stupor. He kept gazing at the ceiling. Whatever had hit Zacharia had happened to him. A silence like that of the dead ensued for a while, and then he said, as though entirely to himself, "They want our blood."

"What?"

....

23 Matan, a mountainous region east of Beirut, which saw heavy clashes between resistance and Phalangist fighters.

"They want our blood."

"Who? How? Why?"

"They took blood from me—by donation, I mean."

Her eyes widened and she was suddenly dumb-struck. Awad continued after a while:

"If only what he'd said had been a little less insulting ... if only they'd asked me my opinion ... if only they'd just humored me and said it was a matter of humanitarian concern ... if only ... if only ... Today they took half a liter of blood; what if they needed a liter tomorrow? Three? All of our blood? What if they needed an eye? A kidney? A spleen? What would we do? Would I be able to say no?"

At the break of dawn Abu Rabih prepared his suitcase and snuck out undetected. His plan was to go to his brother's house in West Beirut and then make his way back to Abu Dhabi from there.

Mariam thought, *Should I do the same? Should I leave everything behind and flee?* But where would she flee to? Her mother was living with three young daughters, all cooped up in a one-bedroom furnished apartment on the tenth floor in one of the refugee buildings. An old building was subject to all kinds of abuse: no elevator; no regular running water and even the staircase was unsafe. Could she go to her husband's brother's house, a man she barely knew? Or to her sister Kawkab's house, where her son, Amer, was responsible for the livelihood of the family?

No one was in any position to bear anyone else's burden these days. Everybody had their hands full with their own problems. She decided to stay and bear her own burden. She decided she wasn't going to be like those three Palestinian men who tried to cross the border into Kuwait by hiding in a water tank. They suffocated and their bodies were later dumped at a rubbish tip.[24] She decided she wouldn't give Rabih reason to taunt her the way Atta, God rest his soul, used to taunt her father. She used to pity his old age and the way his lip quivered, how he cowered into himself every time Atta argued with him.

"You ran away. Had you stayed we would've won," she remembered Atta taunting their father.

"We didn't run, son. We were asked to leave for two or three weeks," he replied.

"You kid yourselves when you tell us that."

"The eye can't fight the awl,[25] son."

"The hand could have extended to the awl with an awl needle. The fathers eat sour grapes, but it's the children's teeth that are set on edge."[26]

"It may have been ignorance, but it wasn't cowardice. Your uncle Ibrahim sold his best cow to buy a rifle, and your grandmother donated all

....

24 This is an allusion to the famous novella *Men in the Sun* by Ghassan Kanafani.

25 A proverb that refers to an uneven distribution of power, where one party is much weaker than the other.

26 This is a biblical proverb from Ezekiel 18:2, which indicates that children inherit the consequences of their predecessors' mistakes and failures.

her jewelry to the fighters. Father Abu Farid used to hide the fighters in the church. Son, the British were on their side, the Arabs were on the British side, the whole world conspired against us, we were weak, on our own, not organized."

"That means nothing to me. Why weren't you organized? You knew since 1936 that the Zionists had their eye on the country. What did you do? You organized a six-month strike and then you slept on silk. You relied on the Liberation Army. The army of seven nations! The Arab army! You slept on the honey of rescue until you got screwed," she recalled Atta's reply.

No, no, Mariam! The situation here is different. Back then the country and the land were ours. We had a right to stay, and the enemy was an antagonist coming from outside. But here, we're refugees. The land isn't ours, nor is the government. No, no! You can't compare the two!

But, *so what if the land isn't ours? Even slaves have better rights than we do. We've been building this country for thirty years, like a plough bull. Factory machines have eaten our fingers. This house was a dump; my and my husband's hard work turned it into a livable home. My mother broke her back picking tomato and cucumber from the fields so they can be sold in the city at the highest prices. My cousin died under the rubble of the building they were constructing in Jounieh, and Therese lost an eye in the nearby silk factory. Jarjoura was buried with his pickax as he was breaking apart the large stones they were using to build those enormous hotels in Bhamdoun and Sawfor for the tourists. We stay here, cold, hungry, in war and peace, building the country with our blood and sweat, our men go abroad, deserting us when a job opportunity presents itself, and we end up living our marriages by correspondence, just to secure a living for ourselves and our children. And they deign to call us 'the foreigners'?!*[27] *No, by God, no! The foreigners are those who leave a country from the first gunshot. Those who run away to New York, Paris, London and elsewhere. Those who strike it rich at our expense and go off to spend their money on trivialities in foreign lands.*

Keep philosophizing, ya Mariam. Your words are as empty as air bubbles.

Mariam kept resisting despite all the pressures. Stung by an insult here, or struck by a gloating stare there, she maintained her silence, and her patience. She put up with Deek, who had come to behave much like an actual rooster, overseeing a bunch of hens whose roosters were absent. Her hair would stand on end every time she heard his voice, and she'd break into a cold sweat whenever she sensed that he was going to stop by her door. God only knew how she was able to defend herself against his many

27 Lebanese arch-nationalist discourse branded Palestinians as "foreigners" (*al-ghuraba'*). In 1979, on the order of Israeli military generals, the Front for the Liberation of Lebanon from the Foreigners was formed. It was an Israeli-state sponsored militia operating as a Lebanese militia and was responsible for a series of massacres and car bombs in the early '80s.

attempts. Maybe because there was an easier hen he could force his manhood on, or maybe because he didn't have an active manhood, limiting him to lustful stares and obscene jokes only.

"Im Awad! You have to leave this house and go and live with your daughter-in-law. Also, tell Mariam that the boss has decided that all the houses in the camp are the property of the Party.[28] We decide who gets to live in them and who doesn't. And besides, her house is big; you two can share a room. We will be bringing families from Damour[29] to live with you. Tell her also, that we have some conditions she has to accept before we let you stay. You can't have any relations with anyone in West Beirut, for example. If you love the folks there, go to them, but you can't have a foot in the West and a foot in the East. That's prohibited."

Im Awad did not reply, nor did it appear that the orders surprised her. He moved a few meters and stopped outside another door. Im Awad gathered her seventy years, along with a few of her things, and headed to her daughter-in-law's house. When she knocked on the door, she heard Rabih's voice, negotiating: "Me ... me ... Let me open the door." She crouched, and when Rabih opened the door

....

28 The Lebanese Phalangists.
29 An area inhabited by Lebanese Maronite families, displaced by Palestinian fighters in southern Lebanon.

he leapt into her wide-open arms. She tickled him and he laughed as he writhed in her embrace.

Im Awad told Mariam about the orders. Mariam said nothing and forgot to ask her mother-in-law to stay for lunch, or even a cup of coffee. When Im Awad got up to leave, Rabih grabbed the back of her dress. His mother shouted at him. He looked at her in surprise. It was very unlike her to speak harshly to him. He started to cry and kicked the ground with his little feet. She ran to him, hoping to console him, apologizing for what she had done. He didn't calm down until she promised him a new racing car and a big box of Chiclets.

Mariam did not sleep that night. She had long thought about leaving that damned camp, but she had always reasoned that in spite of its unfortunate history, it was still the only place she really knew. In its alleyways she jumped rope as a child, and along the road to the convent was where she showed off whenever she could afford a new dress. Behind Abu Shibly's bakery was the first time she felt that strange mix of fear and pleasure when Halim, the scoundrel, squeezed her nipple. It was above the threshold of this door that she slammed the dough,[30] releasing herself from the burden of spinsterhood. It was in this room that Rabih shouted his first cry. Then there was all the effort she had put into

....

30 This is a custom in which a new bride sticks a flattened and decorated portion of dough above the front door of the house, indicating her rite of passage from unmarried to married life.

making the apartment beautiful, year after year. She had planted that gardenia the day Rabih took his first step. And it was because of the gardenia that she slapped his hand for the first time, when he tried to break one of its branches. She had hit him without thinking, and moments later she broke into tears, wishing death upon herself. Then there was the grapevine, stretched on a makeshift trellis. By God, it was beautiful and lush with leaves.

Her mother used to say that the year they left Palestine, the olive trees had given in abundance. It was the most giving year they had ever seen. Remembering this, Mariam wondered, "What am I lamenting? My father used to own land that's bigger than this entire camp, and he left it all behind. He was afraid of what the colonizers would do. He preferred the safety of his children over anything else. He would always say, 'A child's fingernail is worth all the olives, wheat and grapes. Money comes and goes, but the son of man, once he's gone, he doesn't come back.' Oh, Baba, you lost two of your children for nothing—not fighting for oil or olives."

A few hours later and Mariam was packing whatever she could carry into a taxi owned by one of her neighbors. They took off to West Beirut. She wasn't alone in this. There were other families in the same circumstances that had left before her, or would leave after her. The families gathered in the Sanayeh Garden. They lived in tents made of blankets and bedsheets until some of the escaped fighters took over one of the construction sites of a building that hadn't been completed yet. The refugees then took shelter in the building, and it came to be known as a refugee hovel.

The refugees of the Acare building were the last to arrive out of the convoys that emerged from that camp after it fell into the hands of the Lebanese militias. Very rarely do politicians or journalists mention that camp when enumerating the suffering of the Palestinians during the Lebanese civil war. Was it because it was a very small camp that fell quickly to the Phalangists? Or was it because the number of casualties was small compared to the other camps? Could it be that it didn't have anyone to cry over it, as Im Awad would say?

Mariam's luck saw her secure a room on the second floor to share with her one and only. A mother with three daughters took the other room. The middle child was the same age as Rabih. In the third room was an elderly couple whose children were all grown up and long gone. Im Awad took the fourth room. Everyone agreed to share the large living room and kitchen. Mariam thanked God that Abu Rabih was in the Gulf and not with them. His presence would have made things awkward. She didn't contact any of her relatives. And when her brother-in-law came to visit them, she let Im Awad know the contempt she felt for Abu Rabih.

"Forgive me, Aunty Im Awad, but your son has no shame. If it weren't for keeping face, I would push him down the stairs the next time I see him. He should be ashamed of himself. He acts like we're not his flesh and blood. Even strangers have come to see how we are."

"He has his reasons, my daughter. The matter is out of his hands."

"It would've been more dignified if he had pretended that he didn't know what happened, rather than spring this pale visit from his brother on us in his stead."

Im Abdo kept paying the building residents visits for days.

"Good people, we have to organize our commons so that what befell others won't befall us. We have to keep this building in order so it doesn't become like every other refugee building. We don't want it to turn into the Jammal or Boutaji buildings, do we?"

"You're thinking of creating a local government, Im Abdo?" Jamal said, derisively.

"You shut your mouth. Nothing comes out of it except lame jokes. Why don't you and your likes form a government then? Show us what you've got."

"No Aunty Im Abdo. You know better when it comes to governance."

Im Abdo created a women's council. She collected a mandatory payment of a few liras to secure regular cleaning for the entrance and the stairs. She issued warnings to neglectful mothers about letting their children mess about in the lobby, and threatened those she caught littering with a fine.

"Al-fadi ya'mel qadi,"[31] some said jokingly.

"Maybe she should replace Abu Amar,"[32] someone else said.

"Leadership is not for amateurs," said another.

But when it came down to it, everyone respected this sixty-something woman's initiative. If it weren't for her, the place wouldn't have been clean. There was barely any graffiti on the walls, and no one left bags full of trash outside their apartment doors. Better still, people could use the lift.

The refugees got used to their new home. The children enjoyed city-living with what it had to offer of elegant storefronts and sidewalk cafés, each filled with people from all walks of life. The elderly, however, complained about living in sardine cans and reminisced about their days in the camp.

"I do miss the old days! It was enough just to stand out in front of your house to keep yourself entertained. Every passerby stopped, said hello, asked about you and your loved ones, told you a story or a rumor. We were all one big family,

....

31 An Arabic expression whose literal translation is, "Whoever is free can become a judge." It is used to mock people who take on community responsibilities without being asked.

32 The leader of the Palestinian Liberation Organization, Yasser Arafat.

entertaining each other. Days passed without us feeling their heaviness."

"May God punish those who were the cause ..."

"Aunty Im Awad, there is no use complaining. The camp is not Palestine," Mariam would reply.

And then it was the fourth of June.

War planes filled the Beiruti sky.

Worried heads peeked from the windowsills.

Schools dismissed their students ahead of time.

Mothers rushed to pick up their children.

Nervous movement, congested traffic and insistent drivers with hands perpetually stuck to car horns.

Homemakers wondering out loud who the intended targets this time would be.

"They hit Madineh Riyadiyeh."

"They hit Fakhani."

"They hit Sabra and Shatila."

They came back on the second, third and fourth days. Their raids became more vicious. Radio stations broadcasted their own wishful thinking. One gloated about Beirut and its people, and another spouted unrealistic propaganda about the ability of the fighters to resist the onslaught. Conflicting news and deflationary rumors circulated. Sandbag banks arose at every junction and in front of every building of importance. Military jeeps patrolled the streets and alleyways, day and night. Ambulance

sirens blared without rest and voices over megaphones urged people to donate blood, or shouted in
anger to demand that people get out of the way, or
shot rounds in the air, for the same purpose.

They blocked the capital from access to the
south.

They bombed the Qadi bridge, the Aswad
bridge, the Damour bridge.

Others speak of heroic confrontations in Saida
and Ain el-Hilweh, and at the Khaldeh bridge and
at the Na'meh, and about surrenders and betrayals
here and there.

And so, the Beirutis realize that the matter is
bigger than a simple retaliation for the attempted
assassination of an ambassador in London.[33]

Abu Rabih returned from his estrangement determined never to go back again.

"It's enough this time, we're protected by the
grace of God. Life ends and the work never does. I
need to be with the chicklets before they leave the
nest." He wanted to settle down and take pleasure
in Rabih's childhood and see him grow into a man
whom he'd call, one day, "Abu Awad."

He returned on the third of June, the evening
of the attack on Beirut. He was grateful to God for
having arrived before the airport closed.

---

33 Shlomo Argov, the Israeli ambassador to Britain, narrowly
   survived an assassination attempt in London by a
   Palestinian gunman on June 3, 1982.

He was pleased with the building his family had settled in. It was large and had very strong foundations. Twenty bombs couldn't take it out. No war plane can destabilize this pillar. He'd bang on it with his fist, verifying his belief. The place was better than any of the basements[34] in the nearby buildings. And on the other hand, the Israelis care about public opinion; it's impossible that they'd bomb this building. There's a hospital east of here, and the mayor's house is to the west. No, no, it's impossible for them to target this building. Beirut is full of buildings. Why would they target this one?

Rabih lived totally unaware of danger. His mother instilled a deep-seated sense of peace in him by being herself an exemplary model of calm. The bombs and warplanes failed to frighten him, so long as he could jump into the security of her arms. She did her utmost to fulfil all his wishes, even when all the city's shops had sold out of their merchandise. She'd see a brief cease-fire as an opportunity to get Rabih his treats from the only store in town that still had supplies. And on the days when the bombing was ceaseless and she was unable to leave, she'd sigh and say out loud, "My poor darling, he went to bed upset. There was no Pepsi or ice cream today."

"This woman's crazy! With everything that's happening to us, her main concerns are Pepsi and

---

34 A building's underground basement was used as a bomb shelter during the war. Even to this day, the word for a building's basement (*malja'*) is "shelter," as in "bomb shelter."

ice cream for Rabih!" He'd mimic her, saying, " 'My poor darling, he went to bed upset.' Who cares if he went to bed upset? So what? It's embarrassing, Mariam. The world is going to hell and all you care about is running after Rabih's behind!"

"Keep holding up the pillar, my darling. If you let go, the ceiling will collapse on our heads."

Her derision didn't offend him; it secretly made him smile. He was impressed with how calm she was.

Where does she get the ability to transcend the present like that? How can she live like nothing unusual is happening? She welcomes our neighbors who live on the upper levels to come and hide in our apartment. She makes them coffee, if she has it. She distracts Rabih from what's happening outside. She tells him the stories of Shater Hassan and Ali Baba. She diverts his attention when he insists on going out to the balcony. She makes up for what he is missing out on by making him paper boats and planes. She never forgets to check on the evening's supply of candles, batteries and aspirin tablets.

"You can't weigh more than a sack of flour. Where do you get all your abilities from?"

This romantic tendency, concealed in derision, moved her. It was, after all, the only form of romancing he was good at.

"It's because of you, my rock."

Beirut's visitors increased day by day. They came from the suburban outskirts and from the camps.

Families as well as solitary members from various militias. People were everywhere. They filled the offices, banks, mosques, churches and building lobbies. The city was like a honeycomb that had been assaulted by a boy who'd destroyed its peace. Beirut did not complain. It did not reject its people and their guests; on the contrary, it opened its arms to them. It tried to draw them into her, to protect them from evil and harm. Even Hamra abandoned its nightlife to embrace those who sought asylum. The number of families in the Acare building doubled. Every family took in another. Most were relatives from nearby suburbs. They came from Damour, Na'meh, Chawyfat, Hay el-Silam, Burj Barajneh, Haret Hrayk, Ghobayreh and others.

The days passed, the nerves frayed and daily needs became more and more difficult to secure. Austerity in Beirut reached new heights daily. Siege by relatives was as painful as Sharon and his tanks.

"They say they're stomping on the loaves of bread that were smuggled through Mat-haf."

"They confiscated the gasoline that was headed for West Beirut and threatened to set the driver on fire if he tried to bring it in again."

"The war is on some people and not others," Im Yaqoob said, as she watched one of the militia men carry loaves of bread to his relatives.

"If he had any decency, he would have shared the bread with all the neighbors. Screw him and the gun he's carrying."

"Last night I paid twenty-five liras for a loaf of bread," Abu Talal said.

"And I swear I searched the entire Hamra and couldn't find a single bottle of water," Abu Samer said.

Talal's voice burst out, melodiously singing the phrase that was hanging over the electric pole: "We are holding on here. We are holding on here, despite the great destruction." Samer's voice responded, "Oh, Job! Oh, Job!"

"We are holding on! Holding on," and the signature said "Job." Words that the Beirutis and their guests read and sometimes reacted negatively to, and sometimes positively, but in the end, they were always nothing but Job.

But it seemed that Mariam's Job was impatient, for her heart was filled with worry as she listened to the news of their fast advance. She cursed the resistance and all its fighters.

"Saida has fallen ... they[35] detained ... they burned ... they kidnapped ... they betrayed ... they arrested ... they gathered the people on the beach ... They brought in masked informants to identify members of the resistance among those gathered ..."

Mariam became hysterical. She placed her hands on her head and began to pace in circles, like a raging bull. "The dogs, the piglets, they hide behind a gunnysack. The cowards, they act like bats in every war—they only come out at night."

....

35 The Israeli army.

The play was always the same. As though the war had fixed rituals, none of which could be bypassed. It didn't matter if the war was a big or small one, whether it was between two real enemies or between two brothers fighting over some pale inheritance. The tradition was the same. The son of Adam is the son of Adam in every time and place; as a winner he is haughty and as a loser he has to endure the haughtiness of the victor. The dogs who secretly betrayed their own people and collaborated with the victor hid their faces behind gunnysacks.

Mariam was already familiar with the gunnysack. She first encountered it years ago, when the camp fell into the hands of a right-wing militia. It happened on a wild, stormy January night. Nature poured a deluge, along with lightning and thunder from the sky, so much so that one could no longer discern the storm from the killing.

A deluge of gunshots, the sounds of artillery and the whirring of tanks ...

Mariam took her time heading to the bomb shelter when the shooting first began, thinking it was just another short skirmish, as often happened. She didn't want to frighten Rabih, and besides, she thought her kitchen was relatively safe, and that they could shelter in it until the parade was over. Except it wasn't a passing parade this time. The bombing intensified and the gunfire escalated. When she realized that she might be wrong, she scooped up Rabih in a blanket and ran to the nearest shelter.

"Shelter? What shelter? It's a rabbit warren." Mariam squeezed her way through the elderly women who made room for her.

"It's a pity! He is an only child and his father is abroad."

The sound of artillery. The sound of thunder. Children screaming in terror.

"Oh God, have mercy on us!"

The sound of church bells from a distance.

What's the meaning of these bells at this time of night? She learned later that they were Morse code messages sent and received by the antagonizing forces.

After a long night of fear and anticipation, and with the preliminary threads of the daylight of the thirteenth of January, the voices over megaphones sirened their way into the camp inhabitants' ears, demanding that they congregate in the soccer field. *No one is exempt from these orders! Anyone found evading them will be shot without warning!* Murmurs spread, questions, prophecies.

They invaded the camp.

The mothers poured out in shock, hurtling with their children and some blankets, and headed to the designated place. The men were silent and stunned and the women were like cats whose young had been threatened in a way they cannot defend against. The armed men yelled, scolded, scorned and ordered. One of them assaulted a young woman in the name of searching her for weapons. Another, older man, intimidated the women by shouting obscene threats. Another's greedy fingers searched between the breasts of elderly women for what they might have hidden there.

"The women on the right and the men on the left," the megaphone ordered.

The January wind was harsh, but the heavy rain had stopped, as though the sky had mercy on the heads of the wretched who were now stripped of everything but betrayal. Mariam tried her best to keep Rabih sheltered from the cold, drawing him to her chest, assuring him that everything was going to be fine.

A gang of armed men paced the lines, stared in the faces. Some of them wore balaclavas. One of those masked men picked people by tapping them with the corner of his shoe and ordering them violently to go to the front of the line. A large number of men were now at the front. Another masked man came and focused on a few of them. When Mariam looked up, she saw that Abu Saliba, a seventy-year-old man, was one of the men who had been selected. The masked man hit him with the base of his machine gun. "Your children … Where are your children?" Abu Saliba did not speak a word. His eyes were bulging, and his knees buckled under his thin body. He collapsed. Two armed men grabbed him and threw him away from the queue.

The adolescent boys, on whose faces stubble had not yet grown, were separated from the rest and ordered about with insults and scorn.

At midday, those congregated were still standing in the open air, enclosed by the sea from the West and the snow-capped Mount Sannine from the East. It looked like news of the camp's demise had traveled. Relatives, friends and voyeurs came—perhaps just to watch, or to gloat, or to lend a helping hand.

Im Elias, a large, robust woman, stepped forward. "I'm Lebanese. Here's my ID."

"Lebanese? What are you doing here, you bitch?" He grabbed the ID from her hand and ripped it to pieces. Im Elias began to wail and slap her face, so he kicked at her with the heel of his boot and yelled, "I'll drown you in your own blood if you don't shut up."

She inhaled her tears and sobbed as quietly as she could. She sobbed in this way for many more months after that.

Rosette tapped Mariam, who was sitting next to her. "I smell a fire." It wasn't fear that she spoke with but a mix of bitterness and disgust. She dug her nails into her thighs until they almost bled.

Around twilight the congregation noticed an increase in the militia's comings and goings. Murmurs spread.

"The bishop ... the bishop ... the bishop is here to intercede on behalf of his followers. It looks like he might have succeeded, somewhat. The skid loaders have come to a halt."

Mariam managed her own worry and distress by occasionally consoling Rabih, squeezing her mother-in-law's hand or stealing a look at the dwindling front of the line. She heard someone's name being called out and realized that the person concerned had been blessed with a relative or friend who interceded on his behalf and got him out of the line.

She preoccupied herself with Rabih. She calmed him down whenever signs of displeasure emerged. The child beside him was calm and showed next to no objection to his situation, which was quite unlike Rabih. Mariam could see how well the child understood the danger they were all in. It was an astonishing thing that Mariam would talk about every time the memory surfaced.

Exhaustion appeared on her face—Rabih had never left her embrace even for a moment.

"Give him to me so you can take a little break," her mother-in-law said.

"He's sleeping now."

"I should go and try to talk to them."

"Shhh!"

"My legs are as stiff as a dry twig."

"I know."

"Let me try. What's the worst thing that could happen?"

"What happened to Im Elias."

"But this isn't fair."

"They will let us go eventually."

Her name was called out. She was surprised and her heart started to beat as if out of her chest. She thought about ignoring the voice but her mother-in-law made the choice for her and yelled, "Yes! Yes! On our way," and, turning to Mariam, she whispered, "Come, my daughter, let's see what the story is."

Stumbling forward with the young boy in her arms, she was worried by his wheezing— maybe he'd fallen into ill health. Im Awad followed her. A man in civilian clothing tried to take the boy from her, but Rabih woke up alarmed and clung to his mother.

"Thank God you're safe, Aunt Mariam!"

She lifted her gaze to see a slim twenty-year-old with placidly melancholic eyes. She inspected his face for a moment and then:

"Charbel?"

"How are you, Aunt Mariam? Do you recognize me?"

"Of course! How could I not recognize our hunting spear?" The nickname made him smile. A reference to how slim and tall he was, it had been given to him when he joined the factory.

"I've been asking about you for hours. I didn't know what to say to them. I'd say 'Mariam,' and they'd say 'there are twenty Mariams in the camp.' I'm sorry I don't know your family name. Then I said I wanted to find Mariam who used to work in the silk factory, well built, a little older, got married only two years ago. A woman overheard me and said that's Mariam, Awad's wife."

"You're making me laugh, Charbel."

"Who do you have with you?"

"My mother-in-law and my neighbor."

"Come with me." He walked over to the armed man in charge of the queue and whispered something in his ear. The armed man looked over at them disdainfully and then nodded his head in acquiescence. Charbel turned to the women and signaled for them to follow him.

"You are a good man, Charbel. How come you remembered me?"

"Our friendship isn't cheap to me, Mariam. I can still taste those spinach samosas you always made."

"You are a good man. May God bless you. Others have forgotten much more than samosas."

"Anything bad happen to you?"

"We're alive."

Mariam and her companions were now behind Charbel. He tried to walk alongside them and asked Rabih if he was afraid. Rabih buried his face in his mother's chest.

"Tough times, and they will pass."

"May God bless you, son," Im Awad said. "God willing, we get to celebrate with you on your wedding day."

"I am waiting for Mariam to have a girl. She promised she'd be my mother-in-law."

Near the entrance of the camp, Mariam said, "Thank you, son. May God bless you with all that is good. We'll be fine from here on. We need to go back and check on our houses."

"No, no. I won't leave you here, that's impossible. Come with me until things go back to normal."

"We're grateful, Charbel, but we have to go check on our houses, and then whatever is going to happen to the others can happen to us."

"Is that really what you want?"

"Yes, son, it is."

"As you wish, Aunt Mariam. Whatever makes you comfortable. I'll ask Deek to look out for you. He's from our village. I'll come by to check on you tomorrow."

He left them to head back to the Office of Armed Resistance, where he had been hours earlier. He got into an old Volkswagen and the sound of its engine overpowered the commotion from the human traffic returning from the queue.

After that night the camp was no longer what it had been; some houses were burnt, others demolished and more were looted and destroyed. The walls were spattered with obscenities and curses, replacing the revolutionary slogans and aphorisms that had once been there. Armed men patrolled the streets, screaming and shouting at each other for no particular reason. A handful of families, including Mariam, her son and mother-in-law, stayed despite the flood of wrath that had descended upon them.

At night, when Mariam was sure the armed men had gone to sleep, she would listen to the resistance radio station. It was then that she learned that the militia that had been in the camp before the attack had now fled and split into three factions.

"Poor kids. What do they know about war and machine guns? They're just a bunch of high school students. And what do they know about retreats? They probably got hunted like rabbits. God only knows how they died. The broadcaster said that they were tortured, their corpses desecrated."

One of the survivors who arrived in Ras Beirut said that Maroun, nicknamed Ibn Wadfa, was handed over to a butcher, so he could chop him up. Why? The broadcaster added, "Because his name was Maroun, and anyone whose name was

Maroun deserved the most heinous of torments.[36] He betrayed the name he was given. From radio station to radio station, Mariam followed a trail of news, looking for information no one could give her. She wanted to know what happened to Atta. He was going to graduate as an engineer by the end of that year.

Mariam did not see the sixteen children, between the ages of fifteen and seventeen, who were taken from the school grounds and dumped at the front of the church steps, their bodies naked, not quite sunburnt. Their hands were tied behind their backs, some had their eyes wide open, others had their faces mutilated. Most of them did not have a mother or sister to cry over them. Those whose mothers or sisters happened to be nearby were denied by them, like Peter had denied his teacher. As the bodies lay on the ground, Asper, a boy their age, circled them. Only a day earlier, Asper could have been sitting next to any one of them at school, sharing a *labaneh* sandwich or a zaatar *manqousheh*. But today he was there to mutter curses at them, to step on their heads and to give the priest the following orders: "Don't pray over them. Bury them like dogs."

"I lost my mind that day," Im Awad recollected. "I didn't know what I was saying. It was like I was
....

36 Maroun is the name of the saint of the Maronite order to which the Lebanese Phalangists belonged. A minority of Palestinians were also Maronites, but during the war they were considered enemies deserving of additional cruelty.

willing to die. I shouted at the top of my voice, 'You're OK with this, Father? Is this what Jesus taught? Say something, Father! Aren't you a servant of our congregation?' He said nothing and kept his eyes down. 'Why aren't you saying anything?' I said to him. 'Are these the people who crucified Christ?'

"'You brought this on yourself!'" He screamed at me. 'A few childish pranks by a few adolescent boys don't deserve this response!' I replied.

"'A few childish pranks? Is that what you call what Eduar did on Black Saturday? A childish prank? What fault is it of his neighbors if his brother got kidnapped at the river checkpoint? And why didn't Anis take his neighbors into consideration when he assaulted the two youths who were selling the Party newspaper? What about what Yaqoob's grandfather did? Was that a childish prank as well?' He listed every single misdemeanor he could remember and attributed it to us. And everyone agreed with him. No one told him to shut up, no one said he should be ashamed of what he was saying."

"Whoever eats garlic, reeks of garlic, Father."

"In this camp, you turn incense into garlic."

Because the signal from *Thawra* radio station was weak, Mariam had to piece together what might have happened to the Bechara family. Two years earlier, Abu Bechara had bought a piece of land near the camp, after returning from abroad. Everyone was happy for him that day. It was more than a matter of a local man purchasing a piece of land; it was an appreciation of a prodigal son who dutifully and loyally chose to return with the wealth he had made to live among his relatives, near a refugee camp, rather than live where the wealthy do. That day, the families from the camp celebrated and more than one person volunteered to prepare a feast to honor the man who returned from Africa to live among his people. The three-story house he had built east of the camp was the first to be invaded by the militia that fateful night.

Four armed men detained the family in one of the rooms: the mother, father, three boys and their sister, who was barely fourteen years old.

"We need one of you to come with us to search the rooms." He scanned their faces and then pointed at Mervat. "You! Come with me."

Abu Bechara, tongue-tied from fear, stuttered, "I swear, there is no one in this building except me and my kids."

"Vulgar Palestinian!"

"But I'm Lebanese, see ..."

"You can shove that ID up your ass. Where are your weapons? Hand them over."

"Sir, we're peaceful people. We don't have weapons, I swear on my life. We have only been back in the country for two years."

"You came to join in the killing of Christians and the establishment of a Palestinian state in place of the country you sold to the Jews."

Bechara opened his mouth to speak, but the armed man bellowed, "You! Come with us and show us all the ins and outs of this place."

Muffled screams invaded the ears of the detained. Knowing they were Mervat's, the father rushed to the door, but the armed man guarding them beat him to it, returning him to his wife and children an injured man. After some time, which felt like an eon to those detained, the armed man guarding them was called and the militia left the building. Abu Bechara struggled with the door, which was locked from outside, until he could finally open it. And after some efforts at freeing herself of the restraints that were placed on her hands and feet, the mother ran out screaming, "Mervat! Mervat! Where are you, sweetheart?"

She searched all the rooms but found no trace of him. The smell of something burning, something being cooked, drew her to look out of a window on the western wall. She fell to the ground, wailing, "Mervat, my sweetheart, my child, my heart and soul, what have they done to you?"

Hanneh would add to the story by whispering that "Abu Bechara converted to Islam after that." She would say it countless times, and someone would always urge her to "shut up!" The walls had ears and nothing could remain a secret in the camp.

Only a handful of fearful people remained in the camp after its capture—their heads forever bowed toward the ground, afraid of listening to even their own whimpers.

The little one was her only solace in that time. For him alone did she sing and tell stories that his little mind could barely understand. Proudly she told him the story of his grandfather's heroic escape from a high-security Jewish prison, and the story of their escape from their Galilean village to a place on the southern Lebanese border. She told him what life in tents felt like and about the exhausting work she did in a nearby factory when she was barely ten years old. But she did not tell him about the foreman—a man with bulging eyes and a rounded stomach, who continuously threatened the workers.

She was almost twelve the day he asked her to clean the place after everyone left. He came up from behind her. He lifted up her dress. She was filled with tremendous terror and began to scream while he tried to cover her mouth and nose, pushing her into a corner. She didn't know how, by whom or when she was rescued from his beastliness. She remembered poor Salwa as well. Rumors about her death were numerous. Days after her disappearance her body was found washed up by the sea at a place known as Birkat al-Sit. Many theories abound about the poor girl, but Mariam was sure that that beast was the cause. God only knows if that poor girl had thrown herself over a cliff or whether he had thrown her.

❀

Back in the Acare building, Mariam began to wonder where her sister, Kawkab, was, what had happened to her and her children. *Why hasn't she left the southern suburbs to come and see me?* Mariam was now in the heart of the city, which was safer and had greater capacities for withstanding the assaults. If it weren't for Awad and his bad temper, Mariam would have found a way to go see them and bring them back with her by force. *What are they waiting for? For Amer to get killed as easily as his father was? He's just like his father—full of pride and optimism. He differed in one vital way only: Amer is more cautious and has a greater sense of familial responsibility.* She wished he'd stayed abroad, she wished he hadn't interrupted his studies and hadn't returned upon hearing of his father's martyrdom. If only he was willing to live among the families from the camp, who were now in abandoned hotel rooms and apartments of Hamra and Raoucheh. He explained to her why he was unwilling to live there:

"Aunty, I don't think I'm better than them. I'm holding a grudge against them all. I hold them responsible for my father's blood. They are either ignorant or treacherous, I can't decide which. They're the ones who brought the camp to the state it's in. Things could have unfolded in a better way if it weren't for their recklessness and disregard for the value of our lives."

Mariam continued to pace the balcony back and forth without rest. She would look northward, toward the prison, or crane her neck to the right, angling to see into the adjacent street. If only they would come ... *My heart can't bear another catastrophe.* She would periodically place her head in her hands and disappear into a melancholic silence: *How many bitter episodes have you seen in your unfortunate lifetime, ya Mariam? Who are you crying for, ya Mariam? For the brother who was lost in the mountains? For the father whose loss his children lament? For the paternal cousins who were kidnapped by someone from Fateh or Sa'iqa over some trivialities? Or perhaps for Sameh, who was among those taken from the school on the outskirts of the camp? Oh, Mother Mary, please protect Amer. Oh, Mother of Christ, protect Amer!*

A screeching car came to a halt. Her heart beat faster. She looked out, hoping it was them. Except it was another family coming from the southern suburbs—it was the Khatib family, survivors of the Tal al-Zaatar massacre:[37] Im Khalid and her two sons, Wael and Hassan, and her daughter, Abeer.

. . . .

37 A Palestinian refugee camp located in East Beirut. In 1976, during the civil war, the camp was a battleground between Palestinian fighters and right-wing Christian militias. After a long siege, and with people facing starvation, a safe passage out of the camp for civilians was negotiated. However, the Phalangists ambushed the buses carrying the civilians out of the camp. Survivors tell stories of massacres that included cutting out fetuses from their mothers' stomachs and the slaying of women, children, and elderly men.

They were coming to stay with relatives of theirs on the fourth floor. When they reached her landing, she opened the door.

"Thank God for your safety, Aunty Im Khalid."

"God bless you, my child."

"How are things in the southern suburbs?"

"It's an unending battlefield over there. Even the shelters are not safe anymore. Last night they bombed the entrance to the shelter of the Royce. I would have died along with my children, like everyone else who was there, if it hadn't been for Abeer. She refused to go to the shelter—God spoke through her."

"Why are they going to such extremes if they[38] know they're going to win in the end? Why all these heroics? Why don't they[39] surrender to spare our lives?"

"No, my child, the Mariam I know doesn't speak like this."

"My heart can't take it anymore, Aunty Im Khalid. We send every generation that reaches maturity to the slaughter—it's a shame, a shame! We've suffered enough."

"It's what has been written for us, ya Mariam. God's wisdom. We should not object to His will."

She squeezed the elderly woman's hand and said in an apologetic, embarrassed voice, "Forgive me, Aunty Im Khalid. I'm like a woman who's lost her mind."

....

38 The Israeli army and its Lebanese allies.

39 The Palestinian armed resistance and its Lebanese allies.

An ambulance siren accompanied by gunshots frightened Rabih, who ran to hide in the folds of his mother's dress. She consoled him until he calmed down and went back to her lookout. Awad called her in, objecting to the fact that she was putting her life in danger. She sighed. He repeated his calls for her to get back inside.

He wants a cup of coffee.

"Damn him and his coffee," she muttered under her breath.

"The gas bottle is almost empty. How will I make you coffee when it runs out?"

"We'll deal with that if we live long enough."

"Your likes don't die," she muttered again under her breath. "Death is only for the brave. Your kind build roots in the ground, like Noah." She couldn't stand anything coming out of his mouth, not even if he'd said he liked her mascara. All his comments had become unbearable. He, on the other hand, was impossible to impress. He was always criticizing the young fighters: "What are they doing here? The battle is over there and they're here committing petty crimes." *There's no point replying to him because he doesn't listen nor forgive. He wants them to be angels, but they're human being and humans make mistakes.*

"Listen to this," he said, trying to draw her into conversation. "A woman was hit by a stray bullet outside her house on Clemenceau Street. I told you they were useless. We're better off being oppressed by Sharon."[40]

She did not respond. "The coffee's boiled over," he continued. "I can smell it burning. What's wrong with you? Why aren't you paying attention?"

She put the cup of coffee on the table and sat, absorbed in her own thoughts. He tasted it and added, "Your coffee is weak today."

"That's all the coffee beans we had left."

"At this rate, we're facing a famine. Today no coffee, tomorrow without gas, and then ... "

"Let all hell break loose," she muttered to herself.

Why hadn't Kawkab come yet? If only Mariam could go to where they were and bring them back, but there was nothing she could do about Awad, who was stubborn and had already made up his mind against the idea. Should anything happen to Amer, it would kill Kawkab. Poor Kawkab! She lost her mind after her husband was kidnapped. She didn't believe they killed him for a long time after that. They had detained them together that night. They let her go after a few hours but kept him. Everyone who had been detained with them confirmed that he had been killed, but Kawkab lost her mind—both believing and disbelieving. She would give up hope and hold on to it at the same time. Some days she wished she would die. She patrolled

....

40 Israeli Defense Minister, Ariel Sharon, who ordered the invasion.

the beaches every time she heard that a corpse washed up there. She inspected all kinds of corpses: wet and dry ones, bloated and shrunken ones, the clothed and the nude. Everyone was worried about her. She spent months talking to herself in a loud voice, blaming herself: "I'm the reason ... I'm stupid ... I did the wrong thing ... I shouldn't have left him with them. I should have stayed with him ... I didn't do him justice ... I should have pleaded with them ... I should have tried to intervene ... If only I had offered them money ... I'm stupid, and crazy, and a coward. It's a sin around my neck, ya Rafful. May God forgive me for my lack of trying."

Her two daughters and little boy, Nu'man, would cry under the blanket. Their mother had lost her mind.

She stopped going to the church. She considered all Christians responsible for Rafful's murder.

Our sweetheart, Amer, left his studies and came back as soon as they reopened the airport. His return helped Kawkab regain her sanity. Mariam did not sleep that night. She kept listening out for the activity on the street below. Some military jeeps passed by slowly, others sped by. The night passed on but her fears remained the same.

My heart can't take another catastrophe. Oh God, protect us.

The siren of an ambulance on its way to the hospital at the American University in Beirut blared. Someone in the front seat shot a round in the air.

Awad yelled at her, "Get back inside! Get back inside! No one will have time for you if you get hit."

"I wonder how the people are treated over there? Do the militias do the same to them that they do to us?"

"That's enough catastrophizing, woman! Every one of us will get what's written for him in this life. Your complaining won't help anyone."

"I heard you say they've reached the airport. Is that true?"

"No, no, I exaggerated. I was only arguing with Abu Matlaq. They've reached Saida, but what would stop them from advancing to the airport, or anywhere else?"

"Oh God, protect us."

She recounted the number of people who were now under occupation. She wondered where they were going to draw their new borders.[41] At the Ouza'i like their myths say? Will she be able to see her friends and relatives who were now occupied, or will a new Palestine be created between her and them? When will it be Beirut's turn? What will Mariam do to protect Rabih from their hostile faces if they do come into the city?

"Oh God, honor me with a death, any death, a bomb, a sniper's bullet, but don't let me see their

....

41 The Israeli state's borders remain unsettled and are constantly changing due to wars, treaties, and occupations in which more territory is subsumed. Menachem Begin's Herut party, for example, envisioned the borders of a Greater Israel that included Jordan.

scornful faces. What will happen to Rabih if you die, ya Mariam? Will Awad raise him well? Will Awad remarry, leaving Rabih with a stepmother who mistreats him? What if both Awad and I die? Who will raise Rabih then? An uncle? An aunt? A relative? What if everyone abandons him? No ... No ... they wouldn't do that. Everyone would love to have a child like Rabih, especially since he wouldn't be a financial burden on anyone. What his father has saved from his years of working abroad is enough to raise him. No... No... beat the devil, ya Mariam," she said, hoping to distance these dark thoughts from her mind.

She went over to Rabih and embraced him like never before. She ran her fingers through his hair and started telling him the story of Shater Hassan and of Princess Nour, who traveled the seven seas. He fell asleep in her arms and the light from his angelic face filled her with calm.

She stealthily made her way to the fourth floor and congratulated Im Khalid again on getting out alive.

"Aunty Im Khalid, I'm anxious to know how my sister Kawkab is doing. She can't handle another catastrophe. If anything should happen to Amer, it would kill her."

"Ask God for patience, my child. They are in it together with everyone else. God willing nothing but good will happen."

"Amer is stubborn like his father, God rest his

soul. Aunty Im Khalid, do you think that boy has joined the resistance? His father before him did it. In the '48 war he used to work for the Tapline company in Haifa.[42] He left his job, left his bride with his mother in their village and went to join the revolutionaries. When Palestine fell, Rafful fell along with it. His spirits didn't return until the resistance was born."

"Lucky are the people who died before this dark time. At least they died with hopes of better days. You know, Mariam, I sometimes envy my son Khalid, who was martyred on the first day of the siege. He didn't live to see the humiliation we saw during the siege. He didn't see his children writhing in hunger before his eyes. I don't know what else to say. My heart broke to pieces over them. There is nothing harder on a mother in all the world than to see her children hungry. I would have fed them my flesh if I could. Hassan broke my heart whenever he asked for anything, even a rotted piece of bread he could eat. I would bang my head against the wall from frustration. My child, there isn't a Palestinian household left that hasn't had someone kidnapped or martyred from it."

"How long is this freewheeling murder going to go on, Im Khalid?"

"Until God wills otherwise, my child."

"And when will that be?"

....

42 The Trans-Arabian Pipeline, a British-owned oil pipeline extending from Qaisumah in Saudi Arabia to Haifa.

"This is up to His wisdom. We can't object to His wisdom. It was His will that my son and daughter should be martyred and that I should be shot twice and survive. The first time, the bullet hit the jarra[43] and I passed out. When I came to, they were all standing over me. Im Yusuf said to me jokingly, "Blessed ablutions, Im Khalid." The second time I was shot in my shoulder. I didn't feel any pain until I got home and put the *jarra* in the sink, and then passed out. When I woke up, I realized I had a bullet in my shoulder. It stayed there for several months until circumstances allowed me to have it removed ....

"Khalid! My eldest child, Khalid! We hardly knew how we buried him. His sister, Khalida, was among the resistance fighters. When they withdrew to the mountain, she withdrew with them. Khalida was a beautiful young woman, like the heart of day. I wish I could have taken your place, sweetheart. I wish I had married you to your cousin in Palestine. God only knows how she died. Was she tortured? Did she call out yamma?[44] Did she die thirsty? Did she say the Shahada before she passed? Your loss will be in my heart forever, ya Khalida."

Abeer interrupted them. "Yamma, I beg you to stop talking about this. My hair stands on end when I think about those days."

43 A pottery jar used to transport water from nearby aquifers during the siege. Im Khalid would have been carrying one on her head when a sniper shot her.

44 Mother.

A heavy silence descended upon them. Im Khalid broke it when she told them about Wael's explosive reaction to the news that they'd reached the council building in the southern suburbs: "Take me to Abu Amar, and George Habash, and Nayef Hawatmeh.[45] I want to gun them all down."

Im Khalid's voice resumed its own pained and quiet cadence. "When you see what's been done to others, it helps you deal with your own catastrophes. Anyone who's seen how the wounded were wiped out on the streets that lead into Dikwaneh forgets his own personal losses. So what if I've lost a son and a daughter? Entire families were massacred all at once. A whole camp was martyred between Dikwaneh and Mat-haf."[46]

They showed up when she least expected it. She had been preoccupied with trying to get her hands on a loaf of bread. The day before, she miraculously escaped the sudden bombing of Jean D'Arc Street. She was on her way to the bakery when she ran into Im Fouad who told her she had been waiting in line for three hours when the baker came out and yelled,

45 The leadership of the Palestinian Liberation Organization, constituting of Abu Amar (aka Yasser Arafat, of Fatah), George Habash (of the Popular Front for the Liberation of Palestine) and Nayef Hawatmeh (of the Marxist Democratic Front for the Liberation of Palestine), were seen as having failed to protect Palestinian civilians from the massacres.

46 Im Khalid is referring to the Tal al-Zaatar massacre.

"Please, everyone, leave. Don't make me kick you out—we've run out of bread for the day." Im Fouad continued, "All my begging and pleading didn't move him one bit. He didn't even blink at the long list of blessings I rained down on him from the top of his head to the tips of his toes."

Suddenly, they were standing in front of her. Just like that, without introductions, without so much as the sound of an approaching car. They weren't even on her mind when it happened. She showered them with hugs and kisses, and a thousand well wishes and joyful celebrations of their safe arrival. But where was Nu'man?

"Where's Nu'man? Rabih will be very happy to see him."

"He stayed back with the fighters. Last I heard he was in Hay Silam. He's at a joint frontline that's defending the southern suburbs."

"Why did you let him go?" Awad interjected. "They're all just fuel for the fire, pictures for the walls! Those who were much older couldn't hold out for more than five days. Why don't you people learn?"

She winced, but she did not comment. She couldn't stand anything he said these days.

She prepared a place for them in a corner of the large living room and filled it with mattresses, so they could sleep. They sat around and exchanged stories. To avoid responding to his uncle's comments, Amer focused his attention on reading the newspaper. He neither loved Awad, nor hated him. Their relationship was simply that of two men pressed by circumstances to meet occasionally. And even though Awad would occasionally praise Amer for his integrity and sacrifice for the sake of his siblings, and even though he would occasionally play backgammon with him, he nevertheless felt that Amer was a poor companion. An educated nephew like that was useless at backgammon.

The days passed and the battle didn't end in five days as Awad had prognosticated. Slowly, the tension between the two men rose to the surface and became noticeable. Awad had nothing to say except to criticize the flippancy of the armed men: "They roam the streets ... drive recklessly in their jeeps ... terrorize little children by firing in the air... invade the bakeries like beasts and take the loaf out of the children and elderly's reach."

Amer promised himself that he would reply to Awad, but then again, out of respect for his age and place in the family, he swallowed his saliva and muttered to himself instead, "And what have you done, mashallah? If it weren't for my aunt, you would have starved to death. You haven't even contributed a single bottle of water for your child. You're counted as a man because there aren't many men left. If it weren't for Im Amer, I would have taken everyone back to the southern suburbs. Living under the same roof as you disgusts me."

Randa told her mother she wanted to join the Civil Defense for the youth in Bir Hassan. Kawkab objected.

"You want me to sit around here like an old woman, instead?"

"Would you rather you all died and left me here by myself? Of what use would Palestine be to me when you're all dead? We've given enough. Is the revolution ours alone? Let every other family sacrifice like we have."

"Hold on, Im Amer, why would you say that?"

"I'm saying that because of you! Do you think by going there you will make much of a difference? You're afraid of cockroaches—how on earth will you bear looking at blood or treat the injured?"

"You're right, Im Amer. Under ordinary circumstances I would be afraid of cockroaches, but these aren't ordinary circumstances."

"You're delicate, Randa. Your heart is weak. You wouldn't be able to withstand what you might see. People dying, others writhing in agony, some speaking to themselves hysterically, others blaming someone else, and some making final requests before dying. War is not child's play, Randa."

"And because it's not child's play, I have to go and contribute. I'm embarrassed to keep moving from the balcony to the window like this. I have to do something. Something that would make my children proud one day. At least I wouldn't have to tell them that I sat around watching while people died. Please! Tell me 'May God be with you, my daughter.'"

"Ah! Girls are burdens until death!"[47]

"No, Im Amer, I am not a burden. You're overthinking this situation. You know I don't like upsetting you and I have never disobeyed you on anything before. I've been an obedient daughter all my life. Forgive me this time."

Kawkab looked over to Amer. "Say something, son. Reason with her. You're her older brother and now in place of her father."

Amer continued to read the newspaper. It's true that he was a coward but not to the point of denying the courageous their desire to act on their courage. At worst, he would be able to show off his heroic brother and sister in the future. The brother of the hero and the heroine, or, the brother of the martyrs.

Vicious battles took place at the entryways to Beirut: air raids, bombing by tanks and artillery fire at this suburb and that. *Murabitoon* radio station were bombed and stopped broadcasting.

Thawra radio station announced, "The Israeli army is unable to advance one step past Mat-haf.[48]

....

47 The phrase *al-banat lil mamat* was a popular expression denoting that girls were a permanent burden on their families.

48 The Israeli army at one point reached a stalemate at Mat-haf, which was the green line separating Israeli-ally

It's as though the freedom fighters are willing to die before letting the heart of the city be captured."

Local newspapers and radio stations became rife with correspondents—some gloated, others were empathetic. Diplomats and spokesmen came and went. Press conferences were held by this minister and counter announcements were made by that representative. Only a few were left speechless by the unnatural state of affairs. Ambulance sirens blared ceaselessly. Day by day, the air raids became increasingly more brutal.

An unprecedented kind of war was being waged on Beirut and its people. A psychological war—as it was then called. Pamphlets were dropped from airplanes, drifting onto balconies and sidewalks, waking people from their naps. The pamphlets advised the people of Beirut to leave and promised them no harm if they were to take certain roads. The pamphlets pretended to show empathy but concealed a significant threat. For some, psychological warfare succeeded. They believed the pamphlets and fled Beirut. Others were not so lucky—they were caught at checkpoints and what happened to them remains a mystery.

The siege intensified. No water or electricity. Vicious bombing weakened the resolve of some Beirutis. They began to raise their voices, asking the resistance fighters to withdraw. The noose

---

held East Beirut and the Palestinian/Lebanese freedom fighters fortified in the West.

that was around the city's neck had unbearably tightened and holding on was getting harder and harder.

Awad abandoned his theory that the apartment was safer than the basement and he pretended that he was going there at Mariam's insistence. At least in the basement he'd be able to give his ears some relief from the bombing and the ceaseless whirring of the war planes. That day was the worst of the entire siege—seventeen hours of continuous bombing. The basement was filled with the building's inhabitants and even some from nearby buildings. They sat in circles, killing time with conversation and playing cards—theorizing about what's to come. Abu Matlaq gave away whatever was left of his cigarettes, and people divided each cigarette in two, and even the cigarette halves were shared among multiple smokers.

Mariam had only a little left of a loaf of bread. She got lucky several days earlier when she found and followed a military jeep carrying bread for the resistance fighters. She begged them to share some with her. At first, they desisted, but then one of them threw her a loaf, ignoring objections from the others. She saved it for Rabih, hiding it from devouring eyes—she didn't even let Abu Rabih touch it.

Laughter burst forth from one of the corners of the shelter. A group of teenagers, who were collected around Mr. Darwish, were listening to him tell the story of a practical joke he'd played on one of his colleagues at school. They erupted in laughter, like a volcano, when he told them how embarrassed Mr. Said was when he received a copy of *Playboy* via registered mail.

"I was sick of Mr. Said and all his criticism of me. Everywhere he went, he'd call me an atheist and a nonbeliever. He'd say I was Abu Lahab[49] and a corruptor of young minds—I think he might have held me solely responsible for the loss of Palestine, if he could have. I begged him to stop more than once. I asked Mr. Wasef to mediate between us but that only made him bolder and more determined. This was the least I could do to him."

"Did he know it was you who set him up?"

"He was so embarrassed; he wasn't willing to talk about it to anyone. You all know how a dirty rumor grows in our camps—the rumor begets children and grandchildren, and cousins even! But let's suppose he did know it was me. What could he have done? Complain to the principal? Pfft! The principal was just as sick of him as I was."

He went on to share with them the less scintillating practical jokes he had played on the teaching inspector until he too fell in line and stopped antagonizing him.

"I didn't have to do anything. One of my students whispered in his ear that 'Mr. Darwish is a

....

49 Abu Lahab was the half-paternal uncle of the prophet Muhammad and a leader in the tribe of Quraish. A nonbeliever, he fought the prophet and attempted to halt the spread of Islam.

relative of Abu Nidal.'[50] He told him that I was a snake under a stack of hay and God help anyone I set my sights on. That settled my power struggle with the inspector."

Then he told them about the time he pretended to be deaf and dumb at a checkpoint at Bir Hassan, after he tried to speed through it because he was late for class.

"Then there was that time I accidentally pretended to be Ahmad Khatib[51] the day our neighbor Abu George was kidnapped from his home in the southern suburbs. I swear that wasn't my intention; it just happened. I called the office where they had taken him, like a good neighbor, to vouch for Abu George's decency and to say that I'd known him for twenty years and that he has no suspicious ties to any militia in East Beirut. They asked me who I was, and I thought to myself, I'll just give them any name—and so I said "Ahmad Khatib." I swear that that Ahmad Khatib was not on my mind when

50 The leader of Abu Nidal Organization (ANO), a Palestinian political group founded in the 1970s, which was responsible for numerous acts of terrorism against Arab and Israeli diplomats as well as government officials in the Middle East and Europe.

51 A Sunni junior officer who led a split from the Lebanese Army during the civil war and formed the Lebanese Arab Army, which provided support to the Lebanese National Movement and the PLO. Darwish's neighbor, Abu George, would have been detained under suspicion of having relations with militias in East Beirut, for no reason other than he was a Lebanese Christian living in a Sunni-controlled suburb in southern Beirut.

I said that. The man on the other end panicked and he started stuttering, "Yes, sir, as you wish sir. Give me a minute and the boss will be with you, sir." I just kept pretending I was that Ahmad Khatib and my neighbor was released.

"That man is a mobile comedy show," Abu Matlaq commented.

"Uncle Abu Matlaq, you're the closest to the door. Ask your friend Sharon what does he want in exchange for getting him to stop bombing us like this? Tell him that Mr. Darwish, and all the generations he's imparted his pedantic knowledge on, are ready to convert to Judaism—if he'd just stop killing us." A crescendo of laughter and commentary ensued.

"Being Jewish would suit you, Abu Mahmood. You could pass for an Ethiopian Jew!"

"A kippah would look really good on you!"

"Besides, you already call me to light your candles on Saturdays!"

Hysterical laughter from another corner of the shelter. It was Aida—they call her "the Contessa." With her bust thrust forward and one foot against the door, she was blowing cigarette smoke, theatrically.

"I swear she's signaling for me to take her," Adnan whispered with malice.

"Heaven forbid! Shame on you for coveting other people's wares."

"Many girls get aroused when they're afraid. See Amira there, the perfect example of propriety and purity? She slept with that dirtbag, Fathy, just because she was scared. I just need to get her alone for five minutes to put out her tigress's thirst and leave her a kitten. I'd relieve her of that jinn and liberate what can't stay trapped."

"Shame on you, son! Have some respect! We all have girls, mothers and sisters! Don't bite into other people's wares." Adnan blushed and awkwardly went on to join a group of boys betting on coin tosses.

Others whispered to each other, gossiping. *Look who's come down from his ivory tower to join us! Looks like Mr. Raghid has been humbled. He's willing to socialize with lowlife, shelter loiterers like us.*

"As if we're hanging around in bars."

"Tomorrow he'll smoke an *argileh* with us."

"And join us for a game of poker."

"And let us tease him if he loses."

"You gotta hand it to Israel. It's really brought down all the greats a notch."

In another corner, fourteen-year-old Rima was glaring at Amer as she angrily whispered in her friend's ear, "That bastard refused to take blood from me. I went to donate and stood in line for more than an hour. When it was my turn, he said to me, 'Hey, clever girl, you're too young.' Me! Too young! He's the one who's too old." She drew closer to her friend. "But I did get my revenge. I let the air out of all four of his car's tires!"

Im Marwan was telling her story with the deep fryer. "Damned hot oil, it's worse than napalm."

She had been frying some potato chips for her children when a bomb fell on their balcony. Her daughter pulled her from behind and the boiling oil fell on her entire body.

"God bless Amer! If it hadn't been for him ..."

"May God forgive you, ya Amer. The oil would've done Abu Marwan a favor."

Abu Shibli was giving his daily lecture about the benefits of Arak. *Cures headaches and fatigue. A great aperitif. Excellent for dental pain. And helps you get up to your nightly duties. He gave Im Shibli a wink.*

Mariam's heart filled with joy as she observed Alissar and Hassan steal romantic looks at each other, or perhaps a few words of courtship, or a stealthy kiss. *May God keep them safe, so that they may enjoy their youth.*

An intense conversation took place between Abu Rabih and Abu Matlaq.

"If only the resistance would leave before we all get wiped out."

"Don't talk like that, Awad! It's inappropriate. This is a country that took us in, protected us, gave us its youth to fight alongside us. We can't abort mission so easily."

"I don't trust any of them. When the time comes, they'll drop everything and leave. They'll turn their backs on us, the poor people, and leave us to deal with the mess they've made on our own."

"No uncle, please, if you'll permit me," Amer interjected. "According to even enemy reports, these fighters are giving it their all to protect this city. They're fighting an army that all the Arab armies have lost against. They're returning the favor to a city that opened its doors to them, that took them in. If all they were concerned about was their own safety, this whole thing would've ended after the first few days of the invasion."

"'They're fulfilling their duty ... They're protecting the people ...' Pfft! They're protecting their arrogance and pride. Their pride is going to kill us all."

"You're overdoing it, Uncle Awad."

"No, son, I'm not overdoing it. They are! What have they done for us since they started their revolution? It's because of them that we've been displaced from our homes, lost our children and livelihoods. We were better off staying refugees—it would have been safer and more honorable."

"Had we stayed refugees we would have been seen as traitors, as people who willingly sold their lands to the colonizers. We would have remained open to abuse by anyone. You yourself told me about the rumors that the Office of Military Intelligence used to circulate about how cowardly Palestinians were. Have you forgotten the day they spread the rumor that five hundred young men from Ain el-Hilweh got married in one night, because the PLO announced it would conscript unmarried men? I was a little boy then. You have told that story and many others in front of me a thousand times. This standoff and this heroism that you don't like are the actual response of the Palestinians to anyone who assaults them."

"Heroism, standoff, courage, sacrifice ... They're tricking you with these shimmering banners and slogans. You always try and you always fail. You keep retelling the same story from the beginning to no avail. Wasted effort. Why don't you direct your energy to more useful things? If you could spend as much effort on improving yourselves or humanity as you did on resistance, wouldn't that be better? Why don't you aim to be scientists, and artists, and inventors, instead of heroes and martyrs? Look at where the Jewish people were and where they are now. They were the greatest minds of every nation: Einstein, Marx, Spinoza, and, and, and ... As soon as they got distracted by nationalist concerns, we stopped seeing greatness from them."

" ... "

"Tell me, what has the revolution done for you? It killed your father as a young man and gave you the responsibility over an entire family while you were still a boy. It displaced you from your home and ended your education early. Instead of becoming a larger-than-life doctor, you're just a third-rate employee. Other than that, it has made half the Lebanese our enemy, while the other half is on their way to becoming that. Your father would have been alive today had it not been for his obsession with the revolution. He's been obsessed since '48."

"My father wasn't obsessed. He was a hero!"

"And what has become of his heroism? No one in their right mind would have done what your father did in Nabi Yusha.[52] Five wimps with degenerate rifles attacked a base with a hundred soldiers in it."

"And even so, he took over a tank."

"It was a coincidence ... luck. Your father was reckless."

"My father and the likes of him are paying your debt and the debt of others like you. You've spent your whole life in the Gulf, saving money. Have you lived your life even once? Have you ever been a member of an organization? Have you ever been moved by a political speech? Ever rallied behind a leader? Participated in a demonstration? Kissed a girl? Wolf whistled at one on the street? Written a love letter? God only knows, you probably hadn't even been with a woman until the day you married my aunt."

"Shut your mouth, you insolent fool!"

He did shut his mouth and then left the shelter to rent a hotel room that the keeper was unwilling to rent to him until he got one of his foreign girlfriends to be his guarantor. The room, which would eventually house his mother and two sisters as well, cost him twice his monthly salary to rent.

Peculiar was the case of this city. She gave love and tenderness without expecting anything in return. Her streets and cafés might erupt in reaction to

....

52 This is a village in the Galilee region in northern Palestine.

one event today and erupt in a contrary reaction tomorrow. She adopted everyone who sought refuge in her. She gave the foreigner a familiar place and company to the lonely, all while accommodating the debauchery of those high on alcohol and silk.

Peculiar was the case of the Beirutis who under ordinary circumstances avoided greeting their neighbors in the morning, but had abandoned their seclusion and aloofness so that their rich and poor, learned and illiterate, their sophisticated and simple folk, came together to meet the challenges of their existing situation. When the water and electricity got cut off, they headed for the inner belly of the city, extracting water from its artesian aquifers, and they cheated the darkness by buying electric generators, paid for by multiple families. Popular market stalls replaced elegant shop fronts, supplying the besieged with essential needs: batteries, candles, kerosene lamps, and canned food. These were stalls that made light of the bombing, air raids and explosive devices, and unfurled their furnishings along the sidewalks and building entrances.

Where did the young ones learn to transform fear into courage and confrontation? While older people wallowed in their despair, they chased the cautionary pamphlets that fell from the sky, and read them with derision. Johnny would grab one and point it to his rear end, while Ihab would raise his middle finger to the sky, laughing, *Take this!*

What did tomorrow have in store for these young ones? Would they one day regret the courage they once had? Would they one day regret what they were doing and see it as meaningless bravado instead?

A nervous voice blared from one of the local radio stations: "I can't, my dear listeners, explain to you what I'm feeling as I look at this strange congestion at the intersections. After last night's insane bombing, here are thousands of cars returning to besieged Beirut. People are voluntarily reentering the siege. The very day after the harshest day of the siege, the number of cars that have entered Beirut has reached five thousand. All in one day!"

Awad yelled from inside, "Turn off the radio. That macho bastard is broadcasting from seven floors underground. He's disgusting. He's safe and talking on behalf of the people who are in real danger. Sons of bitches, they want to fight with other people's children. If he really is that brave, he should take his radio station and go broadcast from the locations themselves, not from a rabbit warren."

To circumvent his wrath, Mariam lowered the volume.

A woman with a southern accent warned about informants and collaborators with the enemy.

"They are everywhere among us, like bugs in the sacks of lentils from humanitarian aid. At every corner, in a café, at the border of every sidewalk, even at rubbish dumps, they release their poisons. They change their color like geckos, walk in the guise of the resistance, and secrete baseness, and make vile hissing sounds. They purport an exaggerated love of the country, but when the hour of reckoning comes, they take off their masks and reveal their yellow, vile faces. We all know Abu Reesh."

Mariam gasped. She did know Abu Reesh! She had stopped for him and given him alms many times.

The broadcaster continued. "Abu Reesh, known to the residents of Hamra Street and patrons of the Horse Shoe Café in particular. A man with thick hair and beard, dirty and poorly dressed, talks to himself in a loud voice, jokes with people from the neighborhood. Abu Reesh turned out to be nothing but a bug burrowing into the heart of Beirut, its streets and cafés."[53]

It's strange how the tables turn in the blink of an eye. In the days before the invasion, wherever Abu Amar went, people gathered in the hundreds to greet him. Now, what pained the city the most was to see how quickly people would abandon their homes the moment they learned that he was coming to take shelter in their building. The scene repeated itself so often, especially after Israeli air raids regularly targeted the buildings he was rumored to have visited, that this compelled him to take shelter in the back seat of cars stationed in

....

53 An Israeli spy.

abandoned Hamra parking lots.[54]

In the absence of electrical power, the only remaining news outlet was the battery-operated radio, but Abu Matlaq soon supplied electricity to his television set by modifying his car battery. The semiofficial TV station had long become inoperational, so the Beirutis for now had to be satisfied with the TV station of the opposition.

Images of the invaders swimming at one beach or another.

Bouquets of flowers or grains of rice with which their tanks were being showered.

Words of censure, threatening speeches aimed at the Palestinians and their allies.

The head of a militia stripping Beirut and its people of any modicum of humanity: "I don't think there are any innocent civilians in Beirut."

Mariam felt a numbness like death take over every cell of her body but was momentarily shaken out of it by news far worse than the earlier images on the screen. The most right-wing leader of all the militias of the other side announced that he was running for presidential election. That was a blow that she felt was worse than the blow of the siege, the bombing and their victims. Mariam hoped that the matter was only for show and was consoled by the fact that Beirut was surprised and opposed to this nomination.

"This is an insult and provocation to all

....

54 Under the leadership of Ariel Sharon, the Israeli military was intent on assassinating Yasser Arafat by any means necessary.

Lebanese. How can he become a president over all of Lebanon when he has toasted a glass of champagne over the bodies of his own people?"

"Uncle Abu Matlaq, prepare your bindle. We're due for another displacement soon."

"He wishes! He'll never win. His nomination is only for show."

"No, Uncle Matlaq, the man is being paid."

"Never! Are there no men left so a boy like that needs to rule the country?"

"Uncle Abu Matlaq, prepare yourself. It's either the sea or the grave."

"God forbid, man! Ask for God's forgiveness, Abu Mahmood."

The broad smile and the eyes that sparkled with the joy of anticipated victory filled the TV screen. The man began his presidential campaign speech. He threatened the Palestinian who sold his country and came to take Lebanon in its place. He threatened the Lebanese who took the side of the foreigner.

Another militia man now took over the TV screen. This one had once been a defender of Arab sovereignty but was now demanding a military solution to Palestinian presence in Lebanon.

"How do you like this, Abu Matlaq? Our Chamoun[55] is more biased, vicious and harsher on us than their Shimon."[56]

55 Camille Chamoun was president of Lebanon from 1952 to 1958. At the time he presided over all the militias that were allied with Israel during the invasion.

56 Shimon Peres, the interim deputy of the Israel Defense

Abu Matlaq's response shocked everyone. He threw his shoe at the television and shut it off. Mariam looked over toward him, to find his eyes bulging as if they were going to fall out of their sockets. His Adam's apple was moving up and down. Everyone looked at him with shock. Darwish grabbed his arm and shook him lightly at first, but when he didn't reply, he shook him even more. Abu Matlaq remained silent. Everyone who was there began to give their opinion. Abu Matlaq remained stiff as a board. They carried him to the emergency room. He left hours later, having lost much of his memory and the ability to speak properly.

The siege became more vicious and the women of the Acare building made their walkways a place for making *marqooq* bread, conversation and gossip. The basement experienced unprecedented congestion; residents from other buildings began to stay there, and sometimes fighters came to rest for a few hours as well.

Unlike residents elsewhere, the residents of the Acare Building were not in the habit of leaving when resistance leaders came to visit. Had they done that simple and ordinary thing, would they have experienced what happened to them on that afternoon of the sixth of August?

Forces during the Beirut siege, also remembered for his role in the 1948 ethnic cleansing of Palestine.

❈

And then it was the sixth of August.

The siege entered its third month, and Beirut continued on its path along the stations of the cross, alone. Mary Magdalene did not wipe her forehead, nor did Simon stand beside her in silence.

The sixth of August that year was distinguished by a melancholy sun and a dusty sky, quite unlike what we come to expect of August's scintillating suns and laughing skies. August's air that year was humid and heavy, adding to the troubles weighing down on the nervous systems of the besieged—who waited, with something like despair, for someone to speak up on their behalf.

The sixth of August was a quiet day compared to the madness of the days that preceded it. It was a day virtually free from the whirring of warplanes over-head. It was a day the Beirutis had seized to catch a moment's rest. Some left the bomb shelters to check on their apartments, and some made the prepara-tions they thought were necessary to withstand the harsh night they were expecting after the calm.

It was a few minutes after two in the afternoon when Beirut's inhabitants, generally, and the Sanayeh's residents, specifically, heard the sound of yet another air raid.

"Two war planes are circling above the Sanayeh Garden," the radio blurted. The broadcaster hadn't finished her sentence when the muffled blast of two consecutive bombs was heard and felt.

Kawkab felt as if a small earthquake had taken place. The plates and cups on the kitchen shelves shook, and the bed beneath Amer's sleeping body swayed. Azza felt a stranger chill pass through her as she flipped the pages of a magazine. And before the three of them could wake up from their shock, the broadcaster's voice announced that the Israeli Air Force just bombed the Sanayeh Garden.

No, it wasn't bombing. It had actually been only one bomb—an orphan. And it wasn't aimed at the Sanayeh Garden. This was a completely brand-new class of weapon—the likes of which had never been seen before. The radio station corrected its information. The bomb penetrated the heart of the *Acare* building. This is a building inhabited by refugees who fled Phalangist persecution in *Dbayeh* back in January 1976.

Kawkab, her son and daughter hurried to the building to check on Mariam and her family. Before they arrived, by a few minutes, they heard the sound of another explosion.

"It's another bomb. Be careful, son!" Kawkab screamed.

"That's the sound of an explosion," Azza added.

"It's a car bomb!" Amer shouted.

Azza almost fainted when she saw a dismembered limb of one of the injured splayed on the sidewalk. Kawkab restrained Amer, preventing him from rushing toward the trouble.

"You crazy child, there might be another one!"

Amer turned to his mother in shock. There was no building there. There was no shrapnel. The neighboring buildings had not been damaged or hit with any flying debris. The hospital was still exactly in its place. It was as if the building had been an empty cardboard box whose sides had been compacted against each other, when squashed under two strong feet.

One of the journalists commented, One hundred and seventy fatalities ... some stealing an afternoon nap ... some sipping a cup of coffee ... others perhaps having trivial conversations with their spouses ... One hundred and seventy people, among them a mother holding what appears to be an eight-year-old child in her lap ... A relative was able to identify the family of four by recognizing the earrings worn by the mother: they were Rabih, his mother, Mariam, his father, Awad, and his grandmother, Im Awad.[57]

....

57 The Israeli bombing of the Sanayeh building made history as the first time the US-designed-and-made thermobaric bomb was used on civilians. The 1983 *Report of the International Commission to Enquire into Reported Violation of International Law by Israel During Its Invasion of the Lebanon* indicated that over 250 civilians lost their lives in the bombing. August 6, 1982, also marked the thirty-seventh anniversary of the nuclear bombing of Hiroshima.

KHALIL[58]

It's mid-June and Beirut persists in refusing to submit. This enrages them. They attack on all fronts. They target bomb shelters, plant car bombs at the intersection of arterial roadways, demolish bridges, capture loners hanging outside bakeries or natural springs ... they capture Saida ... Sharon's soldiers reach Ba'abda Palace.[59] Some shower them with rose petals and grains of rice. American television announces the imminent surrender of the freedom fighters. Images of prisoners of war fill the world's television screens while Fairuz's sonorous

....

58 Khalil Hawi was a renowned Lebanese poet and scholar
    (1919–1982). As an Arab nationalist, Hawi believed that if
    Arabic-speaking nations were to unite, they could form a
    legitimate political front to resist and overthrow Western
    imperial interests in the region.

59 This is the Lebanese presidential headquarters located in
    East Beirut. It's comparable to the White House in the US.

voice booms across the streets of Hamra, Sanayeh, the AUB square and the Manar corniche.

The echo of her voice dissipates into the wind, like dust.

Alone in his room, exiled from everything but his books and dreams, Khalil awakens from a nightmare. He walks over to his bookcase, eyeing the thousand and one titles in it.

How many times have you deceived yourself, ya Khalil?

Haven't you had enough miscarried dreams?

What has the fire spared of your home[60] and everything you've strived for all your life?

What is it that beats feverishly, tenderly, in the ash-laden grove of your chest?[61]

Yet another June[62] gets a stranglehold on your neck ... Your bridge[63] has been destroyed and your Sinbad[64] drowned by the raging seas.

60 In his writing, Hawi often used "home" as a motif of the dream of pan-Arab democracy and unity.

61 In his poem "Return to Sodom," Hawi writes, "what has the fire spared of my home and everything I've strived for all my life? What is it that beats feverishly, tenderly, in the ash-laden grove of my chest?"

62 Refers to the Six-Day War of June 1967.

63 In his poem "The Bridge" Hawi writes, "they deftly cross the bridge in the morning. My ribs extend to become a firm bridge for them. From the caves of the East, from the swamps of the East, onward to a new East." The poem was set to music by Marcel Khalifeh and became a popular folk song by the same name.

64 Alludes to the poems "the Sailor and the Dervish" and "Sinbad on His Eighth Journey."

Those beautiful eyes, which had once promised love and life on university park benches year after year, flash in his mind. What will he tell her if she asks him about the "Genie on the Beach?"[65] About his firm bridge? What will he say to Alia, Silvia and Andrew, who believe in the new East he promises them in his poems?

Where are those generations of towering, bronze bodies that he built? Where are those whom he trained and prepared in the wind and snow, and in the sun, on embers of sand? Where are those whom he wants to be made of metal, sunburnt, towering and tall?[66]

What kind of tomorrow awaits you, ya Khalil? What will you do when they come knocking? Will you greet them with "shalom"? Will you deny Jesus like Peter? Or will you lower and wobble your head as you're shuffled off with the other captives?

Oh how they will gloat over these optimistic poems.[67]

Khalil, ya Khalil! You have spent your entire life fighting windmills. For more than half a century you've been strumming a guitar with severed strings. For more than half a century you've been trying to rouse a genie ravaged by paralysis. Your dream has died, ya Khalil. It leapt after the sun as it set on the horizon.

....

65 The title of a poem by Hawi that appears in *Banners of Hunger*, a poetry anthology published in 1965.

66 Alludes to "Return to Sodom."

67 Namely, "The Bridge" and "Sinbad on His Eighth Journey."

Snakes and herds of people in dark caves squirm above his head ... the lust of death stiffens him.[68]

It's too late for the ambulance. No resuscitation attempts and no emergency room could save it.

Who are you, ya Khalil, to shield the dream from the flood?

Hey gravedigger, deepen the ditch, deepen it to a bottomless pit.[69]

The neighbor across the hall hears the sound of gunfire. She rushes out screaming, "Dr. Khalil! Dr. Khalil!"

Beirutis suppress their anxiety for a few minutes, just enough to grieve the loss of their poet and his suffering. The newspapers make room for the news which is lost in the folds of graver concerns. A poet apologizes on behalf of Beirut for not eulogizing the owner of the bridge in the way he deserves ... Beirut fails to mourn him in ways befitting the sacred *Flute and the Wind*.[70] The mourning mother[71]

....

68 Alludes to Hawi's "Lazarus," a poem that articulates a state of depression and disappointment following the disbandment of the Arab union in 1961.

69 These lines allude to the biblical Lazarus.

70 The title of a 1961 anthology of poems.

71 Refers to "The Mourning Mother," a poem in which the Palestinian revolution in Lebanon is likened to Christ's revolt against the corruption of his day.

does not cry tears over him. Beirut is busy securing a gulp of water to quench her thirst and a loaf of bread for her chicks.

KAWKAB

At the onset of a cease-fire, Kawkab takes the opportunity to return to her home in the southern suburbs. The roads are grim. Corniche Mazra'a looks nothing like a corniche. Sand hills here. Sand banks there. A car could barely make its way through. The green pine forest is now charred black. "May God blacken their hearts," she murmurs under her breath.

She gasps when she sees the state of Martyrs Cemetery: headstones displaced from the graves they belong to, others destroyed ... some have been dug up. Remains scattered here and there. Dirt and soot cover the marble surfaces that distraught mourners once took care to wash and place flowers on.

The doorman greets her and expresses his happiness at seeing her alive and well. He assures her that he would defend the apartments in his building with his life. She thanks him for his loyalty and tips him with what she's able.

Piles of broken glass obstruct the front door to her apartment. With the doorman and his son's help they force open the door. The glass crunches under her feet. The beastly silence fills her with fear. She ignores her feelings and presses on. An unbearable stench comes from the kitchen. *It doesn't matter, it's just some rotten potatoes.*

The doors to some rooms lie on the ground in pieces. A hole in this wall or that. She doesn't bother with these things. She hadn't come for them.

She walks first into the boys' room. Nu'man's pajamas are in a pile on the floor as if he had only left them there that morning. She picks them up, hugs them and murmurs a prayer of protection, sending its sincerest wishes to her son. On Amer's bedside table she observes a frame containing two photographs, one of her husband and the other for Jamal Abd al-Nasser.

Amer can get angry all he wants; there's no time for hesitation. She grabs the second photograph and throws it in a box she brought with her for this purpose. She opens Nu'man's drawer. Magazines of every kind: *Hurriya, Falastine Thawra, Quds, Hadaf, Muharer, Dirasat Falastiniya, Amal, 'Aamel, Sawt Shaghila* ...[72] She smiles when she finds a copy of Playboy among them.

....

72 This is a list of left-wing political magazines that were in circulation at the time.

This drawer alone is enough to get us into serious trouble. Where did this key ring come from? It's older than Nu'man, actually. I brought it back with me from my last visit to Jerusalem before they occupied it in 1967. She puts the key ring in her bag.

In the girls' room, Kawkab finds that Azza's drawer is locked. She breaks it open with a screwdriver. To her great surprise, she finds newsletters from Amal Organization, others from the Lebanese Communist party, and internal memos from the Popular Front, along with petitions carrying dozens of signatures.

How stupid am I? I've been telling myself all this time that Azza is a good girl, concerned only with her studies. And yet, all of this has been happening behind my back! I'll deal with you later, Azza.

She notices an old newspaper whose pages are so withered they have all but disintegrated.

**Northern Passage into Beirut Still Closed
... a vicious attack at Karantina and Maslakh.
After Ghawarneh, the Dbayeh camp ...**[73]

....

73 Ghawarneh was a small suburb in East Beirut populated by low-wage workers, the majority of whom were Lebanese Shiites who serviced the industrial needs of nearby businesses and factories. They were ethnically cleansed by the Phalangists in January 1976, shortly before the capture of the Dbayeh camp. In the days that followed the camp's fall, the Phalangists committed similar massacres at Karantina and Maslakh, which were also populated by a majority of impoverished Lebanese Shiites.

What's this newspaper doing here? It seems to be as old as Azza. She hadn't even turned thirteen yet. Strange. She didn't look to me like she was affected by what happened. I used to say, the girl is young, she doesn't quite grasp the enormity of the atrocity ... How naive of me to think that. Where did she get this newspaper from? And how did she manage to hold on to it for all those years? May Allah spare me the evils of your surprises, ya Azza.

On the second page she reads a news item titled: "He Rejected His Denomination, So They Killed Him."

"Rafful's friends disowned him ... surrendered him to the butchers ... his neighbors were shocked by what was done to him ... the family refuses to speak about the attempted rapes ... they finished things off by throwing the mother and her children out on the street."

You've reopened old wounds, ya Azza.

Randa, on the other hand, has long ceased to surprise her. And in a notebook of Randa's, whose pages had yellowed, Kawkab reads:

.../1/1976

> *I'm writing this awful event to commit it to memory.*
>
> *I'm writing this awful event so I can learn how to hold a grudge.*

For as long as I live, I will remember that night—I'll remember you piled on top of a seat close to the heater in striped pajamas. With every breath I will remember your cigarette, forgotten between your fingers, its elongated ash falling, causing my mother to rush to clean it up, and her apologizing to our host, "Forgive us, Im Joseph."

I will remember how we deliberated earlier about whether we should or shouldn't spend the night at Im Joseph's house. How we reasoned that our Lebanese Maronite neighbor, a longtime friend of the family, might offer some protection to us, her Palestinian Maronite friends, should the Phalangists come for us.

I will remember the glimmer in your eyes shining with unconditional love and that smile that never parted your lips, not even then.

I live in resentment of you because, when I needed you most, you left me orphaned and confused. I don't forgive you for giving up your life so easily, as though it were yours and yours alone.

Why didn't you run away through the back door? Why did you rush to your fate with such ease? You will probably say, "I did it out of respect for the home I was visiting." To hell with respect for the sanctity of all visited homes! Or maybe you will say "I did it to spare you their wrath," but what greater danger is there than for you to leave me orphaned and confused? Tomorrow, if our paths cross again, I will hold you accountable to the highest degree.

... / 1 / 1976

Who says holding grudges is vile? Grudges are the natural response of someone whose dignity has been insulted. It's the only response available to a dignity that's impotent against the insult itself. It's the split that occurs between the part of the self that's insulted and the part that seeks retribution. They say revenge is the weapon of the weak. Revenge is the law between equals. It's a scream in face of bullies.

God, I don't want your postponed heaven. Cast me into your hell if you so wish, because I am incapable of forgiving you. I don't see any virtue in it. No, forgiveness is nothing but a rotten biscuit that's coated in white sugar. I am only capable of impotent grudges. That's the only response I have to the animal who took advantage of his strength over my weakness and innocence. His viciousness broke my ribs. These will heal one day, but his vile, animalistic behavior, his desecration of my childhood, his obscene, lascivious taunts, his gluttonous eye ... I can't heal from those, no matter how hard I try to "turn the other cheek." God, reverse your commandments. Teach me how to hold a grudge. Make me capable of avenging my childhood, femininity, and humanity.

I will never forget that merciful hand that reached for me and extracted me from the claws of the beast. If tomorrow the clouds of this wild storm part, I will look for him. I will look for him for the rest of my life. I owe it all to him. I will never forget how he circled my shoulder with his arm, nor will I forget his fatherly voice that reassured me, "Don't be afraid, young one. I will bust open that coward's head." He must have had a daughter my age. Why else would he have come to rescue a lowly Palestinian from one of his own men? That bending arm is what protects me from blind hatred. It's there to remind me that there is good and evil, fresh and rotten, the humane and the inhuman, in every basket.

.../2/1976

I won't wear black. I won't announce that I'm in mourning to the world. Not even if you bang your head against the wall, Im Amer. You stupid idiot, you see wearing black as an obligation, a mark of respect for my father. No, you moron, that's not respect, that's acceptance of his death. And who says he's dead? Have you buried him? Have you witnessed his corpse? Has he said his final goodbye to you? Has he already told you, "I'm leaving"? Has he read you his will? Has his killer stepped forward to confess?

Everyone who was detained with him says he was murdered. The bishop, his cousin, your cousin who has contacts there—they all confirm this. Your relative, Abu Wakim, confirms it. But in spite of all their confirmations I won't admit that he's dead. I won't say, "May God rest his soul." I won't wear black. I don't want to close the door on him nor do I want to begin a new page. Start a new page on your own, your future plans are no concern of mine. I will wait and wait until I see him coming, like a green bird, walking and strutting.[74]

74 References the Palestinian folktale of the Green Bird. The grim tale tells the story of a boy slain by his stepmother to replace the banquet meat she ate before the guests arrive.

... / 2/ 1976

Today, among these new neighbors with whom I don't belong, I find myself missing you more. Today, I miss you all: Michelle, Ellie, Roni, Suad and Fahed. Where are you now? Do you remember Randa, the tomboy who used to run with you through the alleyways like the boys? They want me to play like a girl and sit like a girl and to go to school like a girl. I miss you all so much.

We used to steal the figs from the pastor's wife and enrage her. She would run after us, hurling insults as we were running away. We'd pretend we were innocent when she complained, and we'd swear on the Virgin's life and all the saints that we were

Having butchered and cooked her stepson, she offers him to the guests. The boy's sister refuses to eat and instead collects his bones, grinds them to dust and scatters their powder to the wind. Several days later, the villagers notice an unusual looking green bird that speaks. It says to them, "I am the green bird that walks and struts. My stepmother slayed me, my father ate me, and my sweet sister collected my bones." Impressed, the villagers ask the bird to repeat its performance. The bird responds, "I will not comply until this woman," pointing at his stepmother, "opens her mouth." When she does, he fills her mouth with pins and nails. The process is repeated for all those present, including his father, until only his sister is left. When asked to repeat his performance, this time the bird says "I will not comply until this girl opens her hands." When she does, he fills them with sweets, almonds, and raisins.

just playing and didn't mean to bother her. Once, we formed a gang against the other kids in the neighborhood. We named ourselves the Smurfs. We lay in ambush at the intersection that separated their houses from ours and jumped out screaming when they were passing by. We startled the hell out of them and they ran away as if a jinn had appeared.

I miss you. I miss you. I miss you with all there is of yearning, longing, pain and nostalgia.

... / 3 / 1976

In my new school, the girls' school, they refer to me as "the Christian girl," like I was one of the enemies or something. They can't get their tiny heads around the fact that I was almost raped by Christians. It's true—they are deficient in intelligence and religion.[75]

....

75 Refers to a hadith of the prophet Muhammad that appears in *Sahih Muslim* and *Sahih Bukhari,* in which the prophet tells a gathering of local women that he has noticed that hell is mostly populated by womenfolk, and this is because they are lacking in reasoning ('aql) and piety (deen). See, for example, hadith #298 in "Bab Tark al-Ha'id al-Sawm," in "Kitab al-Hayd" of *Sahih al-Bukhari.*

Kawkab

Twelve months have passed since the damned incident and my wounds are still bleeding, not knowing how to heal. The earth has completed a whole revolution around the sun and the bitterness of the experience still lives in every fiber of my being.

One thing has changed though; my grudge against you, Kawkab, has turned into pity. May Allah forgive you. Now I understand that you weren't being harsh, rather, it was the circumstances that made you behave that way. Today, I forgive you, but I won't forget you wailing and repeating that your "girls are burdens until death." You didn't hug us. You didn't console us. You didn't say, "God will make it up to you, somehow." You were simply satisfied with "girls are burdens until death," instead. Why was your motherhood so lacking? Why couldn't you find something more within yourself to give us? Was it stupidity or was it coldness toward us because we were girls? Today I forgive you, but I won't forget how you had the heart to throw us into a pit of snakes. That day I accused you of cruelty, of wanting to rid yourself of the burden we were on you by accepting the offer of one of your relatives to take us in. The home of the snake. Now I know that what you did was out of stupidity, not negligence. May God forgive you for permitting your relative, who was one of their wolves, to take us in.

One other thing has changed in the last nine months: shock has replaced sadness.

I have also begun to notice the little things that happened that night. How, before you left, Abu Amer, you turned to me and looked at me, just me. What did you want to say? Was it a look of goodbye, a look of consolation? Or was it a look of encouragement?

I've begun to feel your absence. I've started to miss you, especially the little things: things like sitting close to you and inhaling your tobacco scent. Like hiding in your bed while you say to Kawkab, playfully, "Where is Randa?" Like hearing your voice blaring at us, "Get up, you lazy bodies, it's almost noon!" Like you are on one of your trips and I am anticipating your return.

... 1/1977

Forgive me, Amer. You weren't able to take his place. You cut short your studies, sacrificed your future and came back to stand by us. I wish you hadn't. Every time I look into your eyes I see an accusation. If it weren't for us, for me, you would have been a hotshot doctor. I wish you hadn't come back.

13/1/1978

Two years have passed since you left. Two years, more than half of which we've spent in a place we thought was a refuge. Two years have ploughed in us all kinds of hardships, but despite their depth they have not lessened the pain we feel for your absence. From the tragedies of Karantina and Maslakh, to the tragedy of the Saad family in Achrafieh, to the massacre of the Selbaaq family in Ain al-Rumaneh, to the siege of Tal al-Zaatar and the execution of its men in front of their children and wives, to the massacre of the wounded along the road to Dikwaneh—all these things should have made my catastrophe in losing you small in comparison. Forgive me, none of these things have lessened my devastation over you, not even a little bit.

I started to read Maw'ed and Shabaka.[76] *I followed news of Faten Hamama and Omar*

....

76 These were popular celebrity and entertainment magazines at the time.

Sharif.[77] I got busy with developments in Iran, where Khomeini's name seems to be rising to prominence in Paris.[78] I listened to news of UFOs. I sat in social gatherings with girls from my class. I distracted myself by sharing gossip and spreading rumors. I preyed on every boy in the neighborhood, until each one of them thought I was his sweetheart. But all the substitutes have failed. You alone remain seated on the throne of my thinking, you alone occupy my mind, my heart and my imagination. Two years have passed and I still expect you to return like the green bird that walks and struts, that kills his butcher stepmother and fills my hands with raisins, almonds, and sweets.

Two years have passed and I still hear you call for me every morning, asking me to make you the best cup of coffee anyone can make. Two years and I still feel your hand on my shoulder every time I fight with Nu'man and my mother takes his side. Yesterday, I almost jumped from the window: a man was walking on the sidewalk on the other side of the road; he had the same droop of the shoulder, the

....

77 Two Egyptian movie stars who were romantically involved.

78 Ayatollah Ruhollah Khomeini began to plot and plan the 1979 Islamic Revolution of Iran while he was in exile in a remote village near Paris.

same manner of flicking his kaffiyeh over his back. Days earlier I almost hugged a man who sat in front of me in a service[79] when the tenderness in his voice sounded like yours.

...10/1978

Today I said goodbye to the school of those deficient in intelligence and religion and joined a classy school in Ras Beirut. What if I hadn't been an A student and the daughter of a martyr? On the way to school, Amer was chattering away. He was dispensing guidance. Playing the father role necessitated by your absence. I didn't listen carefully but one of the runaway sentences caught my attention. "You have to know, Randa, you're not like the girls of Ras Beirut. You're going there to get an education. Don't get involved. Don't start a relationship, don't imitate ... Don't ... Don't ... Don't ..." I wanted to scream in his face, to tell him to shut his mouth, that he had made me anxious.

Leave me alone. I'm fine without your advice and guidance. You're not him ... you will never be, no matter how hard you try.

....

79 Long before rideshare apps like Lyft and Uber, the taxi services on Beiruti streets operated such an amenity, where multiple people shared rides. It was named *service* to distinguish it from the more premium service of a taxi.

Why did you leave me, Abu Amer, to a shallow father like Amer?

.../11/1978

Where did this Wael come from?

He's also an A student, and the son of a martyr, but it's as if he's from another planet. He talks about his tragedies as if they were someone else's.

"I don't hate them, Randa. If we were in their shoes we would have done the same thing. The martyrdom of my father, brother and sister is a natural thing to have happen in times of war. Haven't they also lost fathers, brothers and sisters? They did besiege us until we almost died of starvation, but we were their enemies. Since when do people take mercy on their enemies? They massacred the wounded, but since when have armed men been prophets or Christs?"

"We didn't mutilate the people of Damour like they did with us."

"But all the people of Damour were displaced— the guilty and the innocent alike—and many died just because they were from Damour."

"The revolutionaries executed Hamido because he raped a girl."[80]

"And your hero, Ghassan,[81] *made excuses for him. If it weren't for them, I wouldn't have the chance to go to a great school like this, and meet pretty girls in miniskirts, or to get a good high school certificate at the end of it all."*

...../1/1979

His approach was slow. No yelling, no screaming, and no drum rolls. The feelings grew organically, like the growth of grass in the cracks of a rockface, like the transcendent moment of a Sufi mystic, like the approval of both parents;[82] *that's how Wael came into my life. He's a friend I don't feel shy about undressing myself in front of. A*

. . . .

80 At the onset of Palestinian armed presence in Lebanon, the PLO prosecuted and executed one of its own members for raping a Lebanese woman.

81 Refers to Palestinian writer Ghassan Kanafani, who saw that Hamido's execution was an extreme punishment for an ignorant man and that it did not address the root cause of his behavior, which he saw as the leadership's failure to properly educate and train its members in the needs and conduct of true revolutionaries.

82 In a culture where familial obligations are paramount, to have parental approval from not one but both parents is seen as a blessing.

friend I get nothing other than attentive listening and acceptance from.

We don't plan our dates or romantic rendez-vous. He doesn't recite love poems to me, nor does he delude me into thinking that I'm the most beautiful girl on the face of the earth. He never buys me roses or jasmines. His eyes only look for me and sparkle when they find mine.

Could this be love? But he doesn't turn everything upside down. He isn't all I think about, day and night, like I see in the films of Suad Husni and Faten Hamama. Nor do I have to wrestle with him to maintain my independence and self-determination like a heroine in a Ghada Samman novel. It simply makes me happy when we sit side by side on the school bench, and it disappoints me whenever I get on the bus and find that he isn't there. I am not the woman for whom the sun rises, nor does he worship the ground I walk on, like lovers do in Nizar's[83] poems. He simply expresses annoyance at the school bell whenever it interrupts one of our conversations.

Please permit me, Wael, I won't put a name

....
83 Syrian poet Nizar Qabbani.

on our relationship. I won't give it a title. It appears to be something that languages have yet to name.

13/1/1980

Is it true that you died? Is it true that I'm waiting on a mirage?

How did it happen, I wonder? Did the earth quake? Did the heavens get angry? Was the sun eclipsed in that hellish moment? Did you curse at them, or did they taunt you in the hour of your murder? Did they walk you blindfolded or with eyes open? Did you know the criminal who murdered you? Is it true what they say, that it was your friend, Abu Michel? At any rate, he didn't live much longer that night. A stray bullet did away with his vile life.

Did an image of me, Nu'man and Azza, pass through your mind in that awkward moment? Is it true that you surrendered your soul but that the angels carried you, body and soul, to the heavens? It wouldn't have been too much for you to ascend to the heavens like the saints, because you had a heart that exceeded theirs in love, contentment, and forgiveness. Your only fault was

113

*that you gave up your right to life too easily
and left me to Amer's experimentations.*

*I am not sorry we never found you, because
corpses cannot take refuge. The likes of you
can't be contained by the earth, graves are
unsuitable for them. The likes of you belong
to nature, to the open air, the blazing sun.
The likes of you are bigger than to be eaten
by worms or to turn into dust. The likes of
you are embraced by the sun, whose tenderness elevates them to become stars that light
the world.*

...6/1980

*Nu'man, ya Nu'man! You're all grown up
now, and have opinions to stand by. Mama's
boy wants to join the freedom fighters. Do
you remember the day they came to arrest
our father? Im Joseph hid you among her
own children and said: "Rafful has no boys
here. All his sons are abroad." How happy we
were they believed her.*

*Do you remember the day you and Azza
wrestled and she beat you, even though she
was two years younger? You cried. Im Amer
hugged you and said "My tiny sweetheart,
he took it easy on her. He let her win because*

she's little." You believed her and we laughed among ourselves that day.

Nu'man, ya Nu'man! Do you remember the day they knocked on the door? You hid in the water tank. When we pulled you out, you were all but frozen. We wrapped you in all the blankets our neighbors had to finally get the warmth back into your veins.

My dear Nu'man, in this apartment we no longer have a shared life. Azza and I joined the ranks of "girls" and abandoned you. We betrayed you. We betrayed your childhood. That's why you're holding a grudge against us, always looking for ways to start a fight.

Our childhoods died and their beautiful days ended the moment they ripped us out of that old house whose ceiling leaked every time there was a rainstorm. Here in this apartment that is far more modern, we no longer have mischievous games or get to forge innocent alliances. Here, what's asked of me is to wash the plates and clean the bathroom, and what's asked of you is to go to the store and buy whatever your mother tells you to. The good old days are gone. The days of running after Joseph, Elie and Suad are lost.

*Nu'man, ya Nu'man, the only time we speak
to each other is to fight.*

*How did the good old days end in the blink of
an eye like this?*

Kawkab stops reading.

"You have broken my heart, ya Randa," Kawkab
murmurs to herself. "You've been carrying all this
pain without me knowing."

*It's true, I was stupid. Stupid for thinking that you and
your siblings weren't suffering and because I assumed
that by ignoring the situation, we'd be able to move
on. May God forgive me. I drowned in my sorrow. I
was too busy feeling sorry for myself and I thought
that by calling Amer back I would be compensating
you for the father you lost. May God forgive me for my
stupidity.*

She sobs until it relieves her of the enormity of her
pain. As she enters the living room, she encounters
the large photograph of him hanging on the wall.
On the opposite side, there's a silver sculpture of
the Church of the Holy Sepulcher. A neighbor had
gifted it to her. She thinks about taking it with her.
It wouldn't fit in her handbag. Should she leave it?
She decides to revisit her decision later. She takes
the photograph of him off the wall, holds it firmly

with both hands. His eyes are almost speaking, and it appears as though his lips could quiver at any moment—just as they would have whenever he was agitated. Years have passed with her trying to be sure. All those years and all those confirmations that had come in the form of "May God rest his soul" are now stuck in her throat.

May God forgive you, ya Rafful! We were always second to Palestine in your life. She was always number one. Whenever you faced a choice between us and her, she always won out. Remember, Rafful, remember! I was a newlywed when you left me in the village and went to Haifa, ostensibly to work on the land. You hated working on the land. Farming is deadly. The earth absorbs the body and mind alike, just like roots absorb the soil. Farming is slavery. I wanted a city life ... to be free as a bird ... Not tied to an acre or a plough. I didn't believe it when your cousin Sarkis came and told your mother that you had joined the secret organization and that the English were watching you closely. He said it was possible that you would be fired from your job.

That day you told us, "Sarkis is a coward. There's no difference between him and the ox. His mind is fixed on the plough and sees nothing else."

Remember when you sold my bracelet to buy a rifle? Remember that you never replaced my bracelet. Worse still is that you left me at your mother's house, a new

*bride, while you went around with the revolution-
aries from one village to the next, from one battle to
another.* And I always used to say "Have mercy on
me, ya Rafful. I don't want to be widowed at the
height of my youth. Factor me into your plans!"
And you would reply, "I have another one hundred
years left to live. Tomorrow, when we win, I will
compensate you for all this deprivation. We will
have a dozen children, and I'll make you wish you
were back to these days."

*All the villagers said you were crazy. You and five
others, with useless rifles, attacked a base of fifty armed
men. It's true, I was impressed. It's true that my zaghrouta echoed in all the nearby valleys, but I was also
deeply saddened at the same time. I knew this meant
you would leave us again.*

*Remember the day the mayor came, asking us for
photos to submit with the applications for Lebanese citizenship? You humiliated him. There wasn't a word of
insult left in the dictionary that you didn't pepper him
with:* "Please leave, and don't let the door hit you
on the way out. Keep the citizenship for the people
to whom it belongs. I want to return to Palestine.
All the countries in the world aren't worth a pebble
from mine."

*Your sister's husband left this world resenting you for
how much you scolded him for taking the Lebanese*

citizenship. Do you know how much strife that citizenship would have spared us? And even when I came to tell you that Amer wanted to join a secret organization, hoping you'd scold him and demand he focus on his studies, you, instead, kissed him between the eyes and said, "I support you, son, God willing, your luck will be better than mine."

Even when you did come home for one month every year, it wasn't to spend it with us. You'd go in search of friends of yesteryear—friends from the resistance back in Palestine. One day you'd be in Badawi camp, and another you'd spend in Ein Hilweh, and another in Bass. What else can I say? Why weren't you more careful? Why did you broadcast your thoughts and feelings so publicly and widely? Why did you make an easy target of yourself? Why did you reveal yourself when they asked, "Where is Abu Amer?" You never gave Im Joseph the chance to say a word. "I'm Abu Amer," you said defiantly, and stepped forward. Why didn't you run away through the back door? Why didn't you bend with the storm like many others did? You weren't fair to us, Rafful. May God forgive you, you were unfair, in both presence and absence.

She draws the photograph to her chest and then places it between two layers of clothes in her handbag, not to hide it, but to protect it.

Next, she looks at the bookshelves. *Where did all these books come from?*

She tries to pick up the box, but by now its weight exceeds her capacity to move it. She calls on the doorman for help.

"Take care of this in the best way you see fit, Abu Jamil," she says, handing him a ten-lira tip.

"It will be my pleasure, Im Amer."

NU'MAN

Nu'man dislikes the thunderous whirring of warplanes. When he was little, he used to run and hide in the folds of his mother's dress every time a motorcycle backfired. He was also the first to pile himself into a safe corner whenever unexpected shelling of their neighborhood began.

Nu'man dislikes dying, not only because he loves life, but also because his death will sadden his mother immensely. After his father was kidnapped and never returned, she cried for years. She donned black. She covered her hair with a black bandana and started to age rapidly. She reached a point where she ceased to love them. She stopped spoiling him like before and stopped making him the dishes he liked. She became like Im Bashir's maid—she'd cook and put the food on the table without comment, without begging him or Amer to come back for seconds. She spent years refusing to eat a single sweet. She banned the baking of cake or *knafeh* in the house. True that he did buy his *knafeh* from Arees, but hers had always been better.

Azza is also going to be sad. But hers won't be as immense as his mother's. She'll regret all the fights she started with him. She'll regret ratting him out to Amer, saying that he'd been smoking. Amer was hard on him that day and cut off his allowance. He spent weeks living on nothing but dry sandwiches. He couldn't even enjoy so much as a sip of Pepsi. Azza changed a lot after they were displaced from their rural home in East Beirut to live in the southern suburbs. She started screaming at him to get out every time he walked into her room. She started spending her time reading magazines she hid under the mattress every time her mother came in unexpectedly. The day he threw those magazines over the balcony she shouted, "I hope you die!" She will remember that and cry.

He can't imagine how sad Randa will be, but she will certainly regret looking down her nose at him, calling him "a good-for-nothing dumbass," because she was an A student and he was far from it. It's true that he hated her, but he also showed her off every time a new teacher asked him if he was any relation to Randa. He'd say, puffed up with pride, "Randa is my sister!" But Randa always put him down by saying that she was too embarrassed to have a brother as lazy as him. She will regret every hurtful word she's said to him.

Amer won't be so sad. His death will lighten his load a little. Amer is cold and unfeeling. At this age he still doesn't have a sweetheart or a fiancée. He only knows how to fulfill his obligations. He works like a machine. He has been spending money on the family since his father's martyrdom but he lives in his own world, far away from all their other worries. He never asked him once about his love life, or his work, like big brothers normally would. He never asked him once about how he handles his sexual needs, and he knew nothing about his dreams and ambitions. He did not get angry the day Nu'man announced that he would volunteer with the freedom fighters and that he would go with them to Hay el-Silam.[84] He did not squeeze his hand in encouragement. He stood there, silent and unmoving like the Sphinx.

Will Ibtisam reveal what was between them? Will she come to his funeral? Will she sit next to his mother, Randa and Azza, accepting commiser-ations from the guests like them? He doesn't think so. Ibtisam's afraid of her brother, Ali.

They will pray over him at the Church of Peter and Paul in Hamra. And Abu Maher will say some nice words about him in his eulogy. His mother will break out in tears at every pause. They will bury him in the Martyrs Cemetery. Abu Amar said

---

84 A suburb in western Beirut which was a key front line for Palestinian fighters stationed to defend Beirut against the Israeli advance.

all the martyrs would be buried there. Muslims and Christians. He didn't pay heed to the objections of religious leaders. He said that Christians had become Muslims by martyrdom. He loved Abu Amar but he remained silent, so as not to appear ignorant of politics, whenever the folks of the Popular Front criticized and cursed him. His coffin will be wrapped in the Palestinian flag and his comrades will shoot in the air in salute of the fallen hero. The church will be full of his Muslim comrades, who will make fun of the words being said in a language they don't understand. Some will be irritated by the strong smell of incense and will be forced to leave. Imad and Ramzi will make fun of these big yellow candles that are lit in broad daylight and they'll say, "Candles like these could be a whole month's supply."

When they carry the coffin, the gasps and wailing will increase. His mother will cry out, "Goodbye, my beloved Nu'man, say hello to your father," and she might even faint. Im Jamil might burst into a spontaneous *zaghrouta*[85] and some might follow that with the chant, "Oh mother of the martyr, rejoice, all the children are yours ..." How both beautiful and heartbreaking is the death of a martyr? How beautiful is their eulogy? How

....

85 A ululation that produces a high-pitched sound by the rapid movement of the tongue, usually used by women on happy occasions, such as weddings, to denote jubilation and joy. It may also be used in funerals in defiance of grief and to celebrate the dead.

beautiful is the block of white marble on which his name will be written, along with his date of birth and the statement that he was martyred defending Beirut in 1982?

He feels like he is on the verge of tears, not because of what is about to happen but because of this equally beautiful and bitter melancholy. Like music.

If they came to know what goes on in his head every now and then, would they still consider him a martyr? What if they found out that sometimes he regrets volunteering, and that when danger is at its worst, he wishes the war was over, even if the revolutionaries weren't the winners? And what if they found out that last night he was pretending to be sick to avoid participating in the attack on the Khaldeh Triangle that claimed the life of Hani, who took his place? And what if they find out that he prefers to look at pictures of naked women and to read sex jokes more than he likes to read Abu Ibrahim's books.[86] What if they found out that he wouldn't deign to spend money on *Hadaf*[87] so he can afford a copy of *Playboy* instead?

Nu'man is pleased by the fact that thoughts are not like clothes—dirty thoughts don't leave a visible stain.

....

86 Naji Aloush, a Lebanon-based Palestinian political thinker and president of the General Union of Palestinian Writers and Journalists.

87 A political magazine belonging to the Popular Front for the Liberation of Palestine that was published in Beirut.

When Abu Mujahed came along with three of his comrades carrying some spotted clothes, Im Amer did not rise up to greet them eagerly, nor did she ask about Nu'man. Instead, with eyes downcast, she said, "No need to speak. He visited me last night and he said, 'Goodbye, Im Amer.' He made me promise not to be sad, not to wear black and not to stop making *knafeh*. He said my sadness would make *him* very sad, and make his death real."

AMER

The years Amer spent abroad had not been sterile. Estrangement had stripped him of his physical and mental virginity. He discovered, as he developed in its womb, that he was not the only wretch in the world, and that it's not enough for a human to have dreams, land and belonging to be happy. What developed for him, in rapid and brief epiphanies, was a range of existential meanings that differed from what his father had bequeathed him. He came to experience emotions and sensations that were previously unchartered.

They greeted him at Moscow airport. They took him to the room where he would board. The rituals of official reception ended, companions parted. He remained alone that night in a poor room, similar to Raskolnikov's, the wretch from *Crime and Punishment*, who fled its coldness and loitered about by jumping from one train to another.

He began to feel the effects of estrangement. He missed them all—his mother, father and siblings. He regretted not living with his sisters and brother in the way he should have when he had the chance. He was a different kind of brother. A little father to them, maybe. A brother by adoption, if you will. He never joined in on their mischief. He never participated in stealing figs from the neighbor's garden or in annoying her by deliberately making a ruckus under her window. But he *was* the first teacher who taught each one of them how to hold a pencil and write the first letter of their life. And he *was* the one who protected them whenever one of the neighborhood kids attacked.

Even though he longed deeply for the days when things were either black or white, he wasn't bothered by his choice to pursue a shallow and self-serving life. He only felt a slight, passing pinch of conscience the day his personal ambitions won over his obligations to his family. He had been working as an accountant in one of the offices of the revolutionaries and his wage helped him support the large family his father wasn't able to provide for on his own.

"Why didn't you object, Abu Amer? Why did you squeeze my hand? And why was there a twinkle in your eye? It suggested to me that you were perhaps blessing and encouraging this step. Were you really blessing and encouraging me, or was it my selfishness and greed that made it seem that way?"

He roamed the streets, remembering how he used to wander through the alleyways of his quiet hometown, remembering the calming lights that shone from its half-closed windows. An image of Julia sneaking onto the balcony to blow him a kiss flashed in his mind. He felt the pain of remembering how stupid he had been in his relationship with her. The arguments, laughter and singing of drunkards coming from the bars returned him to the present moment.

He saw young men and women heading toward what looked like a nightclub. He remained on the sidewalk, his heart beating nervously, wishing that a woman would appear and grab hold of him and take him to where the others were heading. He continued to wander, coming and going along the narrow, dark streets, stealing looks into the windows, wondering what was going on behind their opaque curtains. He felt as though he were a beast looking for his prey. He wanted to sin, to drag a woman into one with him and for both of them to delight in it together. This time, it was the sudden sight of a woman in a long, pink dress, waving at a man on the opposing sidewalk, that snapped him out of his stupor.

He returned to his room and threw himself on the bed, stripped of everything but his memories.

They attacked from every corner—all the incidents that happened but which could have just as easily not happened. He remembered her sitting across from him at Café Automatique, wearing dark sunglasses that covered half her face. He remembered how she kept looking over her shoulder, worried that someone might see her sitting with a man, even if in a public place.

Images of her as a shy girl, in a wrinkled school uniform, her coarse hair tied in a ponytail, danced through his mind. The shy student whose chin and voice quivered every time the teacher asked her a question. The graduation to high heels. The femininity that began to be formed by round, cherry lips and long, silken hair that filled him with his first lust. The games that fooled him into thinking he was everything to her, followed by her ignoring him and pretending that there had never been anything more between them than the classroom that brought them together as students.

He felt that he hated and reviled her and wondered if this very feeling wasn't a confession that he still loved her. He started to find excuses for her behavior, for, after all, her situation with him was the same for all the women of his country. She was like them all: a bat that could only fly in darkness and secrecy, too cowardly to love and sin and yet too weak to desist from loving and sinning.

I was right to ignore her when I ran into her at her friend's house. I was right to let her flirt with Adel without reacting. I was right when I decided to end my relationship with her.

A beastly rage overshadowed the lingering longing he had for her, but his continued circling over sin that evening soon brought back his feeling that she may have been innocent. "Where is she now?" He wondered. Maybe she's been walking the path of her reactions and neuroses on her own, hoping that he will one day forgive her? Maybe! Who knows?

A pang of longing invaded him again, a pang that lit up like a bonfire, filling his entire body with the memory of her singing, "I loved you in the summer, I loved you in the winter."[88] He saw her glowing, warm and fragrant, generous in her attention and giving. This image of her covered him like a warm cloud, like holy water. He found himself saying, "I'll fix everything. I'll write to her. I'll tell her how I feel. I'll teach her the language of confession. I'll teach her how to love and how to sin."

Bad luck has been with us since the morning. The electric generator broke down while we were in the middle of a precarious surgery on one of the wounded. We scream ... we curse ... we blaspheme ... we call God and his angels to earth ... The man we're operating on now is barely alive, we do our best to patch things with what we have on hand. Joined by an ailing kerosene lamp

....

88 A song by Fairuz titled "I Loved You in the Winter."

and Im Jihad's smile as her hand wipes the perspiration off our brows, we complete the surgery.

That fretting mother whose pleading rips us apart on the inside. She is waiting for us to raise Lazarus from the dead.

"My son. My only child ... My son, save him ... He is all I have left in this world. Everyone else is dead. All of them. They were all killed in Tal al-Zaatar."

Suad, the one who never calls me anything but "the angel of mercy," was hit by shrapnel that left her paralyzed from the waist down. Her face, however, remains beaming with a smile. Her optimism confuses and embarrasses my nervous breakdowns and rage.

Adnan's minced leg.

Doctor Yusuf's whisper over the body of another wounded man: Don't waste your time with him. Internal bleeding.

Im Jihad, who puts up with our anger, screaming and irrationality with transcendent calm that embarrasses my raging agitation and screaming, "What is this chaos, Im Jihad? Where's the gauze? Where are the scissors? Where? Where? Where?"

"Amer, son, how did you manage to spend four years in Moscow without finding a wife?" *She replies without lifting her eyes.*

I remain silent as she continues, "My brother went on a military round for less than a year and came back with a blonde woman with a bloated belly."

"Leave the matter to God, Im Jihad."

"Our neighbor Abu Khaled went away for medical treatment and came back three months later with a second wife."

I open my mouth to respond but think better of it.

What do you want me to say, Im Jihad? Should I tell you that it was written for me to become man of the house before I knew the meaning of manhood, or even had a childhood? Before I even turned seven, my mother would take me to the nearby pine forest so we could collect some dry leaves for her to bake on. If a boy attacked our hens, she'd call on me to put a stop to it. If the butcher cheated her, she'd tell me, "Son, a woman is easy to cheat; go and give the meat back to that thieving, lying ..."

I was the one who paid our accounts with the butcher and green grocer when the wire transfers came from my father. I was the one who begged them to be patient with us whenever the transfers were late. Should I tell you that all I have known of life are its obligations and none of its other meanings? That Amer comes second, third or even tenth? No, Im Jihad, now is not the time for complaints. Let's leave them in the heart, where they hurt, and not out in the open for everyone to see.

I'm jealous of your optimistic spirit. I wonder how many people have been given this gift of angelic purity? You and my father are made of the same clay. You have the same dream. The same Sufi love, which transcends reality and which pays no heed to actual circumstances. A bit like Don Quixote, to be honest.

"Good night, Im Jihad. Do you want me to drop you off on my way?"

"Thank you, son. I'm going to sleep at the hospital. You go, sweetheart, but don't stay out too late. Be ready for tomorrow. God only knows what He has in store for us then."

A pathological feeling of guilt robs me of the pleasure of the bath Azza has prepared for me. In the bathroom closet everything is clean and orderly. I surrender to the warm droplets falling over my body, hoping they might return to me my humanity ... my manhood ... For months now I have been feeling like my body is a worthless adage. Bathing is a boring routine. I wrap myself in the clean towel and watch the traffic on the street below. There is hardly any movement. Just as I throw myself on the bed, I notice his picture hanging on the wall. I feel like he is judging me with his eyes.

"Are you upset with me, Abu Amer? Yeah, you are. I know you. You wanted me to carry a rifle. But who would've raised the children if I had? 'God raises everyone,' you and Im Jihad always say. But God is busy these days. He isn't raising anyone right now."

"They killed everyone in Shatila."

"They slaughtered them like sheep."

"People cover the streets, corpses piled on top of each other."

These are the phrases I wake up to this morning. People in pajamas stick their heads out of windows. Women cover their hair with handkerchiefs in a hurry... nervous steps along staircases... Supplications mixed with curses... Women wailing, men calling on God the Great, and children in shock. Im Adnan's voice rises above everyone else's: "What black day! What has happened to you, sisters?" *She hurtles, bareheaded and barefooted toward the main road.*

"Calm down, Im Adnan. Take it easy. Slow down. Where are you going? There are armed men everywhere."

"I will walk from here to Shatila."

"Slow down, Im Adnan. Be patient."

"Take it easy, sister... God willing, it's nothing."

In Im Adnan's house we sit around a boy who is in shock. He speaks in incomplete sentences.

"They came. They opened fire ... They stopped. Opened fire ... We fell to the ground. My mother fell beside me. My sisters were sleeping on the ground. We were covered with a woolen blanket. I heard my mother moan in pain. She grabbed my hand and squeezed it hard, meaning, 'Don't move.' I waited until they left. I felt nothing. Blood ran from my mouth and nose. My mother said, 'Go get an ambulance.' I tried to hold her hand but I couldn't find it.

I spoke to her. She didn't reply. I lifted the woolen blanket. Left the house. Saw them. 'That one didn't die,' one of them screamed. I ran. I bled while I was running. I got to the main road. A man from the Red Cross carried me to the hospital. I asked about my mother. No one knows."

In the apartment across the hall, Im Rabeh, bare-headed, wild haired, motions left to right with her handkerchief, slaps her cheeks and supplants words with moaning.

"For God's sake, Im Rabeh, tell us what happened? How did it happen?"

"I don't want to talk. I don't want to! What good will talking do?"

"Aunty Im Rabeh, for the love of God, speak," our neighbor, Hala, begs.

She wrings the handkerchief with her hands, lowers her head so that it's almost by her knees and says in an astonishing, devastated voice, "They killed them. They killed them all."

"Who killed them? And who was killed?" *Hala pleads again.*

"They killed them all and left me. Left me by myself."

"Who were they?"

"Witness me! Tomorrow I will return to the camp. I will stay in the camp, no matter how much they persecute and terrorize me."

"Who persecuted and terrorized you, Aunty Im Rabeh?"

"I will stay. I will stay by their side. I will make a cemetery for them and plant rose and basil bushes. The criminals attacked us with machetes and rifles. They had Israeli bulldozers."

In front of Zaher building, I observe a group of tongue-tied men. Their faces bereft of any expression, even fear. A man approaches them. With an empty mouth and eyes that stare at nothing, he steers four children, all under the age of ten, in front of him. He stands in shock, as if waiting to be spoken to. There's no need for words. The blank silence is the biggest message his countenance can deliver.

"Thank God for your safety, Abu Ahmad," *Abu Rafeef finally says. He looks at the children.* "Go upstairs to the fifth floor, your aunty Im Adnan is there."

Abu Ahmad then tells us:

"God inspired me. I had a feeling. I said to my wife, 'Let's go visit your sister in Burj Barajneh, and stay the night there.' She made fun of me. I left her and went. I took the little ones. The older ones stayed with her. On the way we heard gunfire. We hid in the school. We huddled together with the mice inside the library. From a small window we watched people run into the shelters and then saw the gunmen going in after them. I heard Im

Marwan beg them to leave her son alone. They yelled at her. Killed him in front of her. I heard one speak with a southern accent, 'Lebanese people, don't be afraid; we will only kill the Palestinians.' On my way here I saw dozens of corpses, more than ten from the Muqdad family.[89] I saw two elderly people in their pajamas."

No one lifts their gaze to look at Abu Ahmad. No one asks him for the details. Like sinners on the day of Judgment, they all resume the blank silence.

A European woman in her thirties speaks with fear and agitation: "We were busy with treating the wounded. We were in a hurry. 'Quickly,' the doctor told us, 'before the electric generator runs out of fuel.' They came and opened fire everywhere. We threw ourselves on the ground. The barbaric cacophony, the rabid, hysterical movements, the sound of breaking glass, the screams of the terrorized patients ... They opened fire in every direction and at everything. Each one of us thought the bullet was meant for her or him. We'd hear the insult and then the gunshot. So what if we weren't killed? We've already been terrorized to death."

Her voice changes and she mumbles, "I looked

89 Refers to members of a Lebanese Shiite family who were among the victims of the massacre. A significant percentage of the Sabra and Shatila population was Lebanese.

around after they left and found the sweet woman in her fifties who always called me 'daughter.' She was splayed on the floor. Her white robe turned red."

On the third day, the Beiruti newspapers came out draped in black.

The smell of death emanates from both camps ... Some of the corpses have been hacked ... Body parts flung everywhere.

Sabra and Shatila emptied of men: most detained or killed, few flee.

Those detained nears two thousand.

Israeli Forces round-up detainees in Madina Riyadiya.

Attack on Akka Hospital kills ten children, three doctors.

A nurse was raped then killed. The surviving nurse identified the attackers as Lebanese Phalangists. One woman said they were Sa'd Haddad's men.[90]

....

90 The leader of the South Lebanon Army.

Reagan and Mitterand panic.

The Front for the Liberation of Lebanon from Foreigners claims responsibility for the massacre.

AN AUTUMN BLOSSOMS[91]

"The Israeli Defense Force greets you. Don't open fire on us and we won't open fire on you. Abide by the cease-fire and you shall remain unharmed. The ... Is ... raeli ... De ... fense ... Fo ...."

It rings in his head all day long. The sound of their tanks and their chains invade every cell in his body. Rashid tries everything to distract himself from going back to that astonishing scene, but he fails. Unsuccessfully, he tries to silence the caustic insult that strangulates every beat of his heart. And to no avail, he tries to quieten his tortured conscience over the day he left his mother and

....

91 The title alludes to the Fall of 1982. By November of that year, the Israeli army had entered and secured West Beirut, as well as the departure of the Palestinian armed resistance from Lebanon. The perception at the time was that Palestinian armed resistance had been successfully uprooted.

his brother, Awad, and his family, to die in the bombing of the Acare building.

The autumn air is weighed down by a sticky humidity. The yellow horizon increases in paleness. A sad dustiness appears to be eulogizing the world in its entirety. The waves crash heavily like someone who, despairing, no longer sees the point in persevering.

Her voice is metallic, sharp, penetrating his bones. Her love handles wobble every time she moves her mop left or right, arousing his irritation to the point of nausea. *She's so superficial! She'd fill the whole world with distress if a child's foot were to step on her wet floor.*

What if that boy with the wide brown eyes came to him one day and asked, "Baba, why did you tie a white sheet outside the window?"

I hope the earth cracks open and swallows me before that happens. All our defeats have been bitter and humiliating, but this invasion of Beirut lights a raging fire that can't be put out.

It's about time you snapped out of your shock.

Is the shame yours alone?

Yes, yes, yes! It is my shame alone. I could have done something other than hang a white sheet from the window.

Something insane, you mean?

Is there anything sane about what's happening?

If you had done something at the time, you would've ... you would've ...

What's the point of living when my son's two wide eyes and my daughter's chestnut brown hair have no tomorrow? What's the point of living when all I have to bequeath them is humiliation and occupation?

You are neither a military leader nor president of a political faction. You are not even a member of a militia. So why do you blame yourself?

That silent dialogue fails to diminish the incessant whirring that rips its way through his veins, bringing with it a cellular pain that feels like fingernails scraping down a chalkboard. Lips move in front of him. Eyes widen and then close. Oh, how ugly and superficial it all seems.

Feelings he cannot explain boil inside him. He rises up like someone haunted. He walks to the balcony, heedless of her wet tiles. Her metallic voice reaches him as if from the bottom of a well. He won't let her register her complaint. He has ruined the polish on the tiles. The one with the wide eyes and the other with chestnut brown hair run toward him. They hold on to the ends of his clothes. They speak words that don't reach him. Their laughter seems to him to be like the chirping of summer crickets. The laughter disperses momentarily, the wide eyes narrow, their joy doused by his irresponsiveness.

What's wrong with me? Have I turned into a rock, so as not to be moved by these songbirds and their merriments?

❀

Nothing will get you out of what you're in other than a glass of Arak.

A glass, two, thirteen ... And the whirring is still there.

"The Israeli Defense Force Greets ... Remain sile ... su ... rren ... der... the ... Is ... sraeli ... De ... fense ... Force ..."

Some words from his neighbor's radio hijack his attention: "The United Nations ... International Forces ... Visited ... Donated ... Detonated ..."

His neighbor on the opposing balcony waves to him. He mumbles a few phrases. He nods his head, pretending to listen and agree. The whirring circles him and his neighbor. The white sheet blocks his view. They look like rats, sticking out their heads carefully ... worried eyes, overwhelmed by the shock that has taken him over, by the tank chains that he feels trespassing over every cell of his body, by the silent incapacitation that envelops the earth, the sky and everything in between them.

He imagines his students, and this incites even greater upheaval in him than a man whose virgin bride is being raped before his eyes.

Damn you, Khalil Hawi. You were the smartest among us. You were satisfied with half a glass. You spared your soul having to drink all this bitterness. You left before their plague spread to the heart of Beirut. Did you know, I wonder? If it weren't for those wide eyes and the chestnut brown hair... without them ...

This is the hell the prophets speak of.

His neighbor continues talking. The whirring is still there. He is still unable to hear him. Her metallic voice fills him with quietude. She directs her speech to the neighbor. They exchange some phrases. She runs inside and turns up the radio.

What's wrong with her? It's unlike her to turn the volume all the way up.

She goes to him. Shakes him by the shoulders: "Listen! Listen! Listen!"

She draws nearer. She drags him, practically by force, into the living room. She shakes him forcefully. "Listen! Listen!"

"Maktab Tahrir with breaking news ..." It's the same tone of voice that's filled with deceitful optimism and the same dancy music that precedes the news, and which is always incompatible with it. She shakes him with greater force this time and brings her mouth to his ear, screaming, "Listen! Listen!"

And he listens.

"An ordinary looking man, of ordinary build, without any identifying insignia, opened fire on two Israeli soldiers who were drinking coffee at the Daily Café in Hamra. Breaking News. The man disappeared into the crowd. He was lost ... and ... and ..."

He runs towards her, squeezes her in his arms. Her voice becomes warm and her eyes glimmer with a strange spark. The two children run to him and he picks them up with determination and hope. He looks toward the horizon, drops his yellow countenance and adopts in its place the promise of the pure blue sky.

Translator's Note

In world literature, *A Spring that Did Not Blossom* sits on the shoulders of giants by building on the literary styles of its predecessors. It weaves a cogent, coherent novel, through the mosaic of families, individuals, and neighborhood con- stellations—stories of little children, like Rabih who dislikes his grandmother's kisses, and young adults like Randa, elderly women like Um Awad, middle-aged men and women like Awad and Mariam, martyrs like Khalida, Rafful, and Numan, and actual innocent families massacred for no other reason than being Palestinian: Aal Saed in al-Achrafieh, Aal Salbaaq in Ain al-Rumaneh, and young Mervat (which is not the real victim's actual name) on the outskirts of the Dbayeh camp.

A Spring that Did Not Blossom also gives us glimpses into the villainy of small men with a modicum of power—like al-Rayyes in the office of Al-Quwat now controlling the Dbayeh refugee camp, or the aptly named al-Deek (the rooster), who oversees Al-Quwat's administration of the camp. It also shows us, from afar, deemed perhaps less important for once, the men of war and politics: referring to right wing military leaders running for elections and to Yasser Arafat sleeping in the back seat of a car instead of in an apartment building because even a rumor of his presence in a building would make it a target for an Israeli air strike, which is exactly why Banayat Acre was targeted.

Banayat Acre in the suburb of al-Sanayeh—that building in itself is a character we must not forget and that the novel helps memorialize. A building packed with around 400 civilians at the time, bombed with a vacuum bomb—a bomb designed in the United States for the purpose, originally, of flattening the jungles of Vietnam—and it was used on human beings, let alone civilians, for the first time in history on August 6, 1982. That day was also the 37th anniversary of the bombing of Hiroshima with an atomic bomb—another world first. Was that a coincidence or was it symbolic?

In *A Spring that Did Not Blossom* I glimpse the influence of Ghassan Kanafani's telegraphic style of writing—allusion sets the scene, brevity generates a sense of hurriedness—there is no time for details but the details are nonetheless compacted without neglect. Dr. Habib tells you everything you need to know but not a word more, and the result is a beautifully crafted work of art, which also stands as an artefact of substantial historical and cultural import.

Samar Habib

About the author

Dr. Nejmeh Habib is an award-winning Palestinian writer, researcher, and educator. She has been a lecturer in Arabic language and literature at the University of Sydney, Australia since 2003. She is the author of three collections of short stories—*My Grandmother Gives Up the Dream* (2019); *A Spring that Did Not Blossom* (2003); and *And the Children Suffer* (2001)—and has written several academic books in Arabic, including *Literary Critiques: Collected Essays* (2018); *Visions of Exile and Return in the Palestinian Arabic Novel* (2014); *From Australia: Contemporary Literary Faces* (2006); and *Humanitarian Patterns in the Literature of Ghassan Kanafani* (1999).

Dr. Habib is the recipient of the Australia Council for the Arts Award in 2004; the Arabic Heritage League's Gibran Khalil Gibran International Literary Award in 2006; the Union of Palestinian Workers' Award for Excellence in 2013; and the Australian Arabic Culture Center Award for Creative Writing in 2014.

A Spring that Did not Blossom is her first collection to be translated into English.